WOMAN ON THE RUN

The silver Monte Carlo performed a U-turn and began speeding back toward me. Alarm quickly soared to outright panic. I stopped dead in my tracks when the car began slowing down just a few yards from me. When it came to a full stop, I took to my heels, running back toward Casa Loma. But just before I turned, I got one quick glimpse of Sean's head emerging from the door. He was moving swiftly, and his expression went beyond sinister. He looked positively lethal. He *was* lethal—an escaped kidnapper and murderer for all I knew.

I ran as fast as my legs would carry me. The Casa Loma was only a block away. I could make it—but already the sound of hastening footfalls was gaining on me. My high heels, my clinging dress, and the violin case bumping against my body all slowed me down. He overtook me within half a block. I felt hi⬛⬛⬛⬛⬛⬛ my shoulder in a powerful grip.

Jove Books by Joan Smith

THE POLKA DOT NUDE
CAPRICCIO

CAPRICCIO

JOAN SMITH

JOVE BOOKS, NEW YORK

CAPRICCIO

A Jove Book / published by arrangement with
the author

PRINTING HISTORY
Jove edition / April 1989

ISBN: 0-515-09984-8

Jove Books are published by The Berkley Publishing Group,
200 Madison Avenue, New York, New York 10016.
The name "JOVE" and the "J" logo
are trademarks belonging to Jove Publications, Inc.

PRINTED IN THE UNITED STATES OF AMERICA

10 9 8 7 6 5 4 3 2 1

CHAPTER 1

When Victor got me a job at a castle, I thought I'd died and gone to heaven. Me and a castle—we'd go together like Scotch and water, Fred and Ginger, Irene and Vernon. But I soon got used to grandeur, and in the end it was just another nine-to-five job. The castle is called Casa Loma, and it's a spurious medieval affair on the banks of Walmer Road in Toronto. According to the tourist brochures, Major General Sir Henry M. Pellatt built the castle to entertain visiting royalty, but when the hordes of royal visitors fell off, it was turned over to the Kiwanis Club. They run it as a tourist attraction to raise money for their service work, and I conducted tours to finance my education. *Sic transit gloria mundi.*

I came to Canada to study French at McGill University, since Montreal is the second largest French-speaking city in the world, and more accessible (i.e., cheaper) than Paris.

Before I decided to study French, I led a life of noisy desperation trying to get rich in Bangor, Maine. It wasn't just greed, more like an adolescent daydream really. I blame it on De Maupassant's short story, *La Parure*, in which the heroine feels she was born for "*tous les luxes et toutes les délicatesses de la vie.*" That about sums up my feelings.

My guidance counselor said I had an aptitude for languages, so I decided to learn French and become a member of the diplomatic corps. After graduation I hope to live in Paris, eat in fine restaurants, go to parties, follow the performing arts,

1

and mingle with the rich and famous. A tawdry dream, but my own.

Spending the summer in Toronto had the bonus of throwing me into contact with Victor Mazzini, the only member of my family who enjoys that lifestyle. Don't be fooled by the fact that my name is Cassie Newton. Mom is from Milan and felt secure knowing I was staying with her brother, safe from the sex fiends of Bangor, Maine.

I led my last group of tourists through the echoing hall to the front door and bid them adieu. It was four-thirty; the castle closed at five, which meant there wasn't time for another tour, but some of the tourists liked to wander around on their own. During this last half hour, the guides collected in groups to discuss our illegal tips, our plans for the evening, and to sneak frequent peeks at our watches, willing the last stragglers to leave so we could get away a few minutes early.

It was a quarter to five when a new customer came in. There were no blistering glares for this latecomer. He was no tourist, but my uncle, Victor Mazzini, the celebrated violinist. He looked the way a world-famous musician should look. A flap of silver hair hung boyishly over the forehead of a face that was lean, tanned, patrician in cast, but with a touch of alley cat in the eyes. Flashing eyes, black as obsidian, darted over the collection of tour guides in their natty uniforms, down for a quick perusal of their legs, back up to the bosoms, and lastly took a passing glance at the faces.

He spotted me shaking my head at him and walked jauntily forward, arms out, to place a loud kiss on my cheek. Victor has retained his Italian soul, though he immigrated to North America several decades ago to make his career here. He was often away on tour, but kept a permanent pied-à-terre in a chichi condo on Bloor Street, downtown. A nice, safe, semi-civilized little town, he called Toronto. He like the central location of Bloor Street and chose that particular building because it was set in behind a pretty stone church. He didn't go to church, but being Italian, he felt at home in the vicinity. Priests and ministers spoiled church for him.

Victor claims to abhor the second rate, and it's ironic that his own innate taste is so awful. He buys expensive things but manages to imbue them with a carnivalesque touch. The lightweight suit he wore, for instance, came from Savile Row, but with it he wore a dark brown, hand-stitched, silk shirt and a cream silk tie decorated with a brown treble clef sign two inches high.

"Am I going to get a lift home, I hope?" I asked, extracting myself from his perfumed embrace.

"Nope."

"Don't tell me you walked!"

"In this heat? Are you crazy? I'll meet you at my apartment around six," he said. "I have some business to attend to."

"Oh, about tonight."

This was a very special night for Victor. He was scheduled to perform at Roy Thomson Hall. He had his violin case with him, and I assumed he was on his way there to do a last-minute sound check.

"Last time the stupid sons-of-bitches gave me a bum pickup for my fiddle. So what else is new?" he asked, with a hunch of his elegant shoulders and a toss of one long-fingered hand. "I'm driving down to the hall now."

Victor liked to affect an air of ease before his concerts, but in fact there was a nervous tremor in the spread fingers. His black eyes darted around the lobby to where the stragglers stood in groups. One pair recognized him. It wasn't surprising as his picture decorated half the billboards and newspapers in town, heralding the concert.

A tall, muscular man with short, dark hair and a moustache was looking at him with interest. The man didn't look like an afficionado of classical music. Between the Western hat in his hand, the jeans and the leather boots, he looked more like a Willie Nelson fan. I thought the smaller, swarthy man in the blue polyester suit was with him, but as I looked, the smaller man walked away. The tall one nodded and smiled, and Victor nodded back.

Many of these discreet acknowledgments of recognition occurred in Victor's life. He cherished every one of them. If the recognizer was of a forward disposition, the next step was for him to approach and shake hands, maybe request an autograph. The tall man didn't seem to be an autograph hound. He turned and examined an undistinguished suit of armor hanging on the wall.

"Will you be home for dinner?" I asked Victor. He nodded, but distractedly. "What time are you leaving for the hall?"

"Sevenish—the concert starts at eight," he said, looking around, hoping for more recognition.

Victor was a terrible ham. He always had some gimmick going to increase interest in his life and performances. He set down his violin case and pulled out a Cuban cigar about the size of a cucumber and slid the gold paper ring from it.

"No smoking," I chided, pointing to the signs. "*Défence de fumer. Se prohibe fumar. Vietato fumare*—we even have it in Italian, especially for you. Put the stogie back in your pocket, Victor, like a good boy."

"Damned country's becoming fascist. A man can't even have a cigar," he complained, but pocketed it. "Is it permitted to visit the can? That's really why I dropped in. Ever since Doc put me on this high blood pressure medicine, I'm like a leaky faucet. Where's the closest?"

"The employees' john is around the corner. I guess no one will object," I said, pointing down the hall. "Right there, across from our lockers."

Victor dashed off in a great hurry, his violin case under his arm, and I resumed my scrutiny of the stragglers. The crowd was thinning nicely—only six bodies left.

The tall man with the moustache and western hat ambled forward as soon as Victor left. "Pardon me, but wasn't that Victor Mazzini, the violinist?" he asked politely. He had a pleasant voice, deep and rumbling. His eyes were nice too—brown, liquid and friendly as a puppy's. I noticed right away that he was American, and felt kinder toward him, but he wasn't from my part of the country. There was a western twang in his accent.

"Yes, I thought you recognized him," I smiled, waiting to garner a bouquet of compliments to relay to Victor.

"Pretty hard not to. His face is on the back of just about every bus in the city." There was nothing of the puppy in his smile. The brown eyes revealed a hint of the wolf as they flickered over my face and down for a quick assessment of my body. He had that mannerism in common with my uncle. He wouldn't see much. Our uniforms are similar to the Girl

Guides'. The oxfords issued with them are of an orthopedic cut.

I hadn't thought of the cowboy as a wolf at first. He looked too down-home. Wolves should be more stylish, like Victor. This man was just regular folks. He was barrel-chested, with arms like legs showing below his short-sleeved shirt. Construction worker, maybe? My own inclination in men is for successful academics and/or artists; lean men with worldweary expressions and intelligent eyes. Besides, the man's hairline was in danger of receding. It wasn't quite what you could call receding yet, but there was a discernible thinning, a little rounder half moon atop the forehead than nature had originally intended. The moustache was too big and shapeless, too.

I finished sizing up the tourist and said, "He's giving a concert tonight at Roy Thomson Hall."

"That's the modern building downtown—kind of a round glass jar on top?" His smile revealed white teeth, just slightly overlapped in front.

I could strike architect from the list of his possible professions. "Yes, it's a newish building. I take it you're a tourist in town, Mr. . . . ?" I wasn't hinting to learn his name, but it sounded that way, and encouraged him.

"Bradley's the name, Sean Bradley. I'm a damned Yankee. I think you might be one yourself, if my ears don't deceive me?"

"Guilty as charged."

He shifted his weight to one foot and crossed his arms, revealing that he was making himself comfortable for a chat. "Where are you from?" he asked.

"Maine. I'm working here for the summer." He rotated his big hat in circles as it dangled from his fingers.

He had a boyish, open way about him. He looked like the kind of man who would say "Aw shucks, Ma'am." "Interesting place," he said, looking into the Great Hall. "It would make a dandy bowling alley."

I thought I'd heard every possible foolish comment on the existence of a real castle in a modern city. "Yes," I said, swallowing a smirk.

Sean tilted his head to one side and laughed. "Gotcha!" he said, pointing a finger at me as if it were a pistol. The ice broke, and we talked for a few minutes about Casa Loma. When the conversation flagged, Sean said in a voice just a shade too nonchalant to be innocent, "What's there to do at night in Toronto?" A wary light was in his eyes, alerting me that I was going to be invited to join him.

"The usual things—movies, restaurants, shows, music."

"Not much fun doing them alone," he said leadingly.

"That's the trouble with traveling," I shrugged, not encouraging, but not unfriendly either. Being an American, he seemed less a stranger.

"Maybe you'd be interested in showing me the sights?" he suggested.

"I'm afraid I'm booked up tonight. I'm going to Victor's concert." The threat of a violin concert will usually send a man like Sean scampering faster than the word "herpes." I consider violin screeching one of the embalmed arts myself and was only going because I couldn't get out of it.

He put on a considering expression, forehead corrugated. "I wonder if it's sold out."

"It is," I assured him, but didn't mention the spare ticket in my purse. "Are you a lover of classical music?"

"Who, me?" he asked, and laughed his deep, rumbling laugh. "I hardly know a violin from a Fender. That's a gee-tar. I chord a little. But as folks say, I know what I like, and I'd like to spend the evening with you." The look that accompanied this was a frank, friendly, and doggedly persistent.

I thought again about that extra ticket. It seemed a shame to waste it. "I have a spare ticket for tonight. Would you like to meet me there?"

"I feel like a panhandler! I wasn't looking for charity. Let me buy it from you," he offered, a hand already sliding to his back pocket for his wallet.

"That's all right. I got it free from Victor. He's my uncle. My guest had to cancel at the last minute. Wait a sec, I'll get it from my purse."

I was struck, as I went to my locker, with what an ill-advised thing I was doing. I never went in for Kamikaze dating. Till I went to Montreal, I'd always lived at home, and my mother has less than liberal views on relations between the sexes. She's an admirer of Phyllis Schlafly. I hadn't picked up a stranger all summer, but in spite of his wolf act, Sean Bradley had that open kind of a face that made him seem harmless. At least he didn't look like a lecher or pervert, and I didn't have to go home from the concert with him. I opened my locker, which none of us actually bothered to lock. We carried our money in our pockets and just kept our coats and purses and spare junk there.

The guard came out of the men's john while I was at my locker. "Would you mind telling Mr. Mazzini to get a move on? It's closing time," I said.

"Where is he?"

"Isn't he in there?"

"No, it's empty. I'll have to look around for him, Cassie. The Music Room—that's where your uncle would be." He wagged his head as he walked off, turning right at the end of the hall, toward the Music Room.

I closed my locker door and took my purse with me to leave. The other guides were coming into the narrow hallway now, chattering away.

The closing bell chimed as I went back to the lobby. I saw Victor's silver head among the last of the tourists on their way out. He must have gone to the Music Room while I was talking to Sean Bradley. The only ones left now were the little swarthy man in the shiny blue suit and a tall, blue-haired lady.

"Here it is—a good seat," I said, handing Sean the ticket. "The concert's at eight."

"Thanks a lot. Maybe we can go out after and do something?" he suggested.

"We'll see." I waved goodbye and watched him leave. He looked like a football player as he swaggered away, shoulders rolling. A big man, but with an athletic stride.

If we went anywhere after the concert, it would be to the party Eleanor Strathroy was throwing for Victor at her house in prestigious Forest Hill. I had planned to attend the concert and the party with Eleanor's son, Ronald, a Bay Street stockbroker, but he'd been called to Montreal on company business the night before. I'd been going out with him a little that month—nothing serious, or even very enjoyable, though Ronald was an extremely eligible bachelor.

The Strathroys were members of the elite WASP society in Toronto. His mother was very big on charity committees and in social affairs. Eleanor was a widow, and Victor's current squeeze, so I met Ronald through Victor. He took me to all the right places: the Granite Club, the St. Lawrence Yacht Club, and to private parties where I could start training for my future life as a diplomat and sybarite. Caviar, for instance—I could now eat caviar without gagging, and I was learning a little something about wine. He drove the right car (Mercedes), wore the right clothes (tailormade), and spoke good but incomprehensible English. His conversation was about guaranteed investment certificates and longterm annuities and such excruciatingly dull, but no doubt necessary things.

The stuffiness I didn't mind as much as the tendency to show off. He never introduced me as Cassie Newton, but as "Cassie Newton, Victor Mazzini's niece." His dates had to be special in some way. We enjoyed a symbiotic social relationship; he only took me out because of Victor, I only went to get to the places he could take me. There was the added bonus that he wasn't lecherous—in Ronald's case, that was a bonus. You never had to fight your way out of the Mercedes. He was always there to hold the door and walk you to the elevator.

Well, tonight Victor's niece would be going out with a far from perfect stranger she'd picked up at work. If I liked the way he behaved himself at the concert, and if he showed up in a decent jacket, I'd ask him to Eleanor's party afterwards. If not, I'd hitch a ride with Victor.

I got a lift to the apartment with one of the tour guides, and hurried off bustling Bloor Street into the air-conditioned lobby to swish up on the elevator to the seventeenth floor. I enjoyed the elegant building as much as Victor—probably more, since he was used to such things. Victor had a maid who prepared dinner before she left at five. There was a note on the kitchen table. "Cold chick. and salad in frig, buns in oven to be heated. Fruit and cheese and leftover choc. cake for dessert. Enjoy."

About five hundred calories of the choc. cake would be enjoyed before dinner. Nobody should go through life without reading Proust and without trying Rhoda Gardiner's chocolate cake. It was sinfully rich, and definitely addictive. My mouth salivated at the very thought of it. I cut off a wedge, put it on a plate, and headed to the living room. I turned on the radio, then sank down on the sofa and leaned back, kicking off my shoes.

Doleful classical music moaned from the hifi, telling me that Victor had been the last listener. Rhoda liked country and western, and I preferred light rock. I switched the dial and luxuriated with the cake, thinking about the night. When I saw the *Toronto Star* on the coffee table, I opened it and flipped to the Entertainment Section to see what they had to say about the concert.

It was the usual stuff—a rehash of Victor's career, his recent tours, his records, a few references to the more spectacular moments in his life. The time he walked off the stage in Boston due to a noisy audience was, as always, mentioned, along with a comment on his flamboyant affair with the soprano from the New York Met, and a discreet, non-libelous reference to his drinking problem—that would infuriate Victor. He was dry nowadays. Maybe I should hide the paper till after the concert.

In the accompanying picture, he held not his famous Guarneri violin, but a large cigar. His head was cocked to one side, and the famous Mazzini smile flashed. A close examination of the picture showed some resemblance to Mom—the eyes, the wide, warm smile—but Mom was a woman of a certain age and a certain weight and a certain rigid coiffure held in place by lashings of hair spray that robbed her of style.

The article described Victor's violin. It wasn't just any old Guarneri, but a Giuseppe del Gesù. Giuseppe was the greatest of all the Guarneris. One of them worked with Stradivari. In fact, a del Gesù was second only to a Stradivarius. "Like Paganini, I prefer the more robust tone of a Guarneri to the sweetness of an Amati or Stradivarius," Victor often said to the press. I suspect his taste would change if he could ever get his hands on a Stradivarius.

There was also a tantalizing hint of the "surprise" Victor had been using as a gimmick for this show. I had an unconfirmed idea what that surprise might be but hadn't mentioned it to anyone, not even Victor. When the cake and the article were finished, I set the table. We'd have to eat early to allow my uncle to get to the hall on time. He wouldn't eat much tonight, but he'd make up for it later at Eleanor's party. Shrimp and lobster, champagne, caviar—Eleanor threw the greatest gourmet bashes in town.

At six-fifteen, Victor still hadn't arrived. I became a little worried and called the hall, but he wasn't there. On his way home then. He'd grab a wing of cold chicken when he got here and call that dinner. I wished I had his will power, but rationalized that a woman who'd been on her feet all day required more nourishment. I took a peek in his room and saw his tux was gone. It had been there in its plastic bag from the cleaner's yesterday. Actually my uncle hadn't sounded very sure about eating at home. Maybe he'd gone on to the hall already, stopping on the way for a snack. He wasn't a creature of habit. Lord, I hoped it wasn't a glass of wine he'd stopped for, which had a way of multiplying to three or four glasses if the company was convivial. But really he had been very good lately. When he still hadn't got home by six-thirty, I went ahead with my own dinner.

The only worry in my mind as I showered and dressed was whether I'd been wise to give that ticket to Sean Bradley. But a fellow American with those liquid eyes and overlapped teeth couldn't be dangerous. He wasn't really a cowboy, I thought. What was he, and where was he from? The accent wasn't heavy enough for Texas, and the clothes weren't good enough for him to be an oil baron. A school teacher, an engineer? He didn't look like a magnificently successful professional; he'd be a toiler in one of the lesser but still worthy professions. Not one of the world's great men, but he was all right for a casual date.

I brushed my tawny hair out loose and caught one side back with a white nacre barrette. For this grand occasion I had bought a wisp of white raw silk that made my Visa card tremble in shock. It looked like a fancy dust rag on the hanger, but much better on the body. A piece of the material was cut on the bias and draped over one shoulder, giving the effect of a toga, it fit fairly close around the waist, and draped again over the hips. It looked best on a long, lean body, which mine was in the process of becoming on those days when Rhoda didn't bake a cake. It was lean enough that Victor included me in his comdemnation of modern womankind, determined to destroy

God's greatest creation, the female body. He preferred full-figured Balzacian women.

I went back to my room to do my face. I have a bold, mannish face, with a square jaw and a long straight nose that is redeemed from masculinity by full lips. "The lips of a harlot," Victor once said. He tries to be shocking but only sounds quaint. I colored my harlot's lips, put some gel on my cheeks and a brush of frosted burgundy shadow over my dark eyes and was ready.

I picked a mauve mohair shawl and went down to the lobby. The doorman hailed a cab, and I drove off to Roy Thomson Hall with a tingling air of excitement hovering around me. I wondered if Sean would wear a jacket. In the heat of summer, some of the audience would be in shirt sleeves, but there would be no shirt sleeves at Eleanor's party. If he came too casual, I just couldn't invite him, that's all.

Sean hadn't arrived yet when I was ushered to my seat. Inside, the hall is shaped like a horseshoe. The mezzanine and balcony seats curve around the stage and are angled to give a good view. The ceiling is a dazzling collection of acoustical banners, acrylic discs, and stalactites with two big circles of lights in the middle. I passed the time by looking around at the hall and the audience while waiting for Sean. Victor says the acoustics could be plusher, especially for strings. He mentioned a lean, transparent sound, but added that it was "very intimate" for a hall of nearly three thousand seats. I didn't think Sean would be enough of a connoisseur to worry about the acoustics, and I knew I wasn't.

I got there at ten to eight. At two minutes to, Sean still hadn't come. I was disappointed at first, then angry at the waste. The house was sold out, and any of my friends would have loved to get the ticket—or could have been coerced into using it anyway. He'd probably picked up some woman at a bar. Damn! My watch showed one minute to eight. An expectant hush permeated the hall as the audience waited for the lights to dim and the curtain to rise. I waited with the others, feeling an urge to tell my neighbor I was Victor's niece. But first I'd make sure he turned up, and turned up sober. It was eight o'clock now, and the hush was deafening.

CHAPTER 2

The hush was broken by a muted pounding of feet on the carpeted aisle. One did not run in Roy Thomson Hall. Roy Thomson Hall is the kind of place where you find yourself calling a person "one." My head slued around, like everyone else's, to see what ill-bred specimen had escaped the ushers, and quickly turned to face the stage again, pretending I didn't know him when I saw it was Sean. Yet I was glad he'd come. His running slowed to a trot as he drew nearer, his eyes scanning the rows for me. He lifted a finger, gave a kind of salute and a broad smile, and began wriggling his way in past the seated patrons.

He was wearing a jacket and tie, but the jacket wouldn't feel at home at Eleanor's party, and that tie! It looked as if it had been designed by Picasso in one of his more vibrant moments. "Sorry I'm late," he boomed lowering himself into the seat. "Couldn't find the darned place. I was sure I knew exactly where it was, but it moved on me."

"These new buildings are all alike—undependable. One of those big acoustic tiles fell right off the ceiling the week the place opened."

"Is that so?" he asked, glancing ceilingward with a doubtful face. "The show should be starting any minute now."

We both looked expectantly to the closed curtains. The silence could reasonably have been filled by a compliment on my outfit. Sean said, "Was Victor nervous, or have you seen him since this afternoon?"

12

"I haven't seen him. He was supposed to be home for dinner, but he didn't show."

"You live with him, do you? That must make for a lively time."

"Oh, it does."

"I was reading something in the paper about a surprise he has for us tonight. Care to let me in on it?"

"I would if I could, but I can't. He didn't tell me."

"Maybe he's got a new violin," Sean suggested.

I smiled at his naiveté in musical matters. "He never uses anything but his del Gesú. It's a famous old instrument. Kind of like the Duesenberg of violins. I have a hunch about the surprise, but I won't even let myself think it," I added mysteriously.

"Could you let yourself say it without thinking?"

"I think just maybe—but I'm probably wrong. It's really conceited of me to even suggest it. Anyway, Victor's written a little piece of music—he does that once in a while. He slaves over it for weeks, then suddenly plays it as a surprise at one of his big concerts to astonish the world, and lets on he wrote it in a day or something. He's such a ham," I added fondly.

Sean turned a puzzled face to me. "How does that contaminate you with conceit?"

"Didn't I tell you? I think maybe he's dedicating it to me. He's mentioned half a dozen times that I've put him in touch with youth again. I make him listen to modern popular music and take him to the movies he wouldn't go to alone. I've heard little snatches of something I don't recognize floating through the door of his studio. He says it's a capriccio, a free-form piece of music, kind of light and lively. He has a certain mischievous sparkle in his eyes when I ask him what he's calling it. But I'm probably wrong," I added. Yet I was sure enough to have bought the expensive wisp I wore, in preparation to take a bow here at the concert hall.

Sean's brows lifted uncertainly. "I guess that'd be quite an honor."

"It'd be fabulous—like having a poem written in your honor, or a perfume named after you, but I'm . . ."

"Probably wrong," he said, nodding his head, while a

crooked little quirk of a smile moved his moustache. "We'll soon know. It's five after eight. It should be starting soon." We both checked our watches.

At ten after, it was my turn to say the same thing. The audience was becoming restive. The orchestra began playing soft background music to soothe the savage breasts. By eight-fifteen I had spotted Eleanor, waved to her, and pointed her out to Sean as Victor's friend. When Sean lifted his Timex under my nose to show me it was eight-twenty and the curtains remained adamantly closed, I felt guilty and asked him to Eleanor's party.

"I thought we might go out somewhere for dinner," he parried. "You've already supplied the tickets. The least I can do is feed you."

I was already feeling guilty about the concert, or lack thereof, so I shook my head derisively at his unliberated ideas. "You're living in the dark ages. Women are no longer wined and dined as of yore. This time, the treat's on me."

He was uncomfortable at receiving anything from a woman. "Tomorrow it's my treat," he bargained. "You notice how cagily I weaseled my way into another date? Here you thought I was a rube, just because I hail from Nebraska."

"I didn't know you came from Nebraska. I really don't know a thing about you. What you do for a living . . ."

"I sell hardware."

I looked at his face, which mirrored the unspoilt plains of Nebraska. Yes, I could picture that moustache and crooked smile behind a hardware counter in some small midwestern town, those strong hands hefting a wrench or hammer. He would be knowledgeable about "two-by-fours" and "ratchets" and such things. A vision sprang into my head of him putting up shelves in a white bungalow and turning hamburger patties on an outdoor barbeque. All in a flash it came to me, as things do sometimes. I'm not psychic—more of a dreamer really, but snatches of things that never were just pop into my head.

I became aware of a hand waving three inches in front of my eyes. "Hardware—Nebraska," he repeated, frowning at my faraway look. "Threw you for a loop, did it? You mistook me for a brain surgeon? Maybe you were wondering what a hardware type was doing touring a medieval castle. I like old things," he said simply.

The white bungalow transformed itself to a Victorian house with gingerbread trim, in a state of being restored by those same brown hands. "I heard you. I like old things, too." Old masters, old money. "I wonder what's keeping Victor. I hope nothing's happened to him."

"What do you mean—an accident?" he asked sharply.

It was more an excess of wine I actually had in mind, but I said, "He's never been so late before. They'd announce it if he weren't here."

"Do you want to go around to his dressing room and ask?" Sean said. I just knew he'd be one of those men who always wanted to be handling situations. I like the French wait and see philosophy myself.

"Let's wait a minute longer."

In exactly sixty seconds, the large, cheap, ugly Timex was hoisted under my nose again. I was just gathering up my things to leave when the curtain opened and a man came out and bowed. A buzz of excitement ran through the hall. Was it a preamble to the "surprise" we had been reading about? When the noise subsided, the man announced that Mr. Mazzini had been unavoidably detained, and the concert was being post-poned. He went on to explain that ticket holders could receive a refund at the box office or wait to hear the new date announced, apologized for the inconvenience, and extended his heartiest apologies on behalf of the Directors of Roy Thomson Hall and Mr. Mazzini.

Victor couldn't be drunk. He hadn't been overindulging at all, and this concert had meant so much to him. His heart was the next thing I thought of. "A stroke!" I gasped, and clutched at my own heart, which was performing aerobics in my chest. "He's had a stroke! He has high blood pressure, you know. The doctor put him on medication just two weeks ago. Oh my God, Sean, I'd better get to the hospital."

Sean flew into a towering calm. "Steady now, steady," he said, holding my hand in a firm grip. "Nobody said anything about a stroke or hospital. High blood pressure's as common as headache these days. Let's go around and find out what's going on."

"Yes, you're right, of course," I said, trying to be reasonable, but my hands, my whole insides were shaking.

It took us a few minutes to work our way out of the hall and into the lobby. Sean formed a driving wedge through the mass of irate humanity, dragging me behind him. The departing crowd grumbled in well-bred voices and gathered in groups to discuss alternative entertainment, since they were dressed up and ready for a night out.

The most accessible route to the dressing rooms was by leaving the front door and walking around to the rear entrance. At least it was the easiest for me, as it was the only way I'd ever gone. I went up to the first workman I saw and asked if he knew anything about Mr. Mazzini's failure to perform.

The man wiped his brow with his hand and gave us a disgusted look. "He never showed up. Never called the hall—nothing. Are you from the press? I'll tell you what *I* think. I think the guy did it on purpose, planned it for publicity. He'd do anything to get his picture in the papers. Performers—they're all alike."

I weighed his opinion and found it not entirely incredible. It was a fact that the tickets for the fourth and last performance weren't moving as well as Victor had hoped. The first night was sold out, the second and third nights selling well enough, but sales for the last performance were flagging. There were plenty of other things to do on a Saturday night. And Victor disliked playing to anything but a packed hall. Not appearing for the first concert would stir up a lot of publicity and put a rush on tickets for the other nights. He was probably sitting at home smiling to himself at the furor he was causing.

We asked around till we found the manager, and I introduced myself but learned nothing more. Mr Mazzini had not appeared. He had not been to the hall before the concert, though he'd told me he'd be there at five o'clock. The manager was more angry than worried. He didn't say it, but you didn't have to be a mind reader to see he shared the stagehand's opinion.

Sean assumed a strong, take-control manner and asked, "Did you phone his home?"

"Of course we did. We sent a man over at five to eight, and he wasn't there. The doorman hadn't seen him for hours."

"Did you phone the hospitals?" Sean asked.

"Certainly. Every effort was made to find him. Have you any idea how much money is involved in this performance? The tickets sold, a *massive* advertising campaign . . ."

"A man's life is also involved," Sean reminded him, with a haughty stare that surprised me. He took my hand. "Come on. We'll find him," he said confidently, and we left.

"I guess the first move is to go home," I said doubtfully.

"That's as good a place to start as any. I've hired a car. You'll have to give me directions."

It seemed an eternity passed as we waited in line to get out of the parking lot. We didn't talk at all on the way home, except for my giving Sean directions. I was wrapped up in my own worries, and finding his way through the traffic seemed to occupy Sean's mind. When we drove into the underground parking garage at the apartment, I spotted my uncle's car in his personal parking spot.

"He's here! He's back!" I shouted.

"Wasn't his car here when you left?" Sean asked.

"I don't know. I don't come this way. I use the front door, but he had his car at Casa Loma this afternoon."

Sean parked in a visitors' space and we went into the building and up the elevator to the apartment. The door was locked, but I let us in with my key, calling Victor's name as we entered.

I hurried in, pushing light switches as I went, but I already knew he wasn't sleeping, or sitting in the dark. I knew he wasn't there, and felt sick with apprehension. Everything looked exactly as I had left it. The indentations of the pillows on the ornate Italian provincial sofa were mine. There were no fresh cigar ashes or butts in the crystal ashtrays, no wineglass, no Victor.

"He must have been here. Where can he be?" I asked.

"How about that doorman downstairs in the comic opera uniform?" Sean said. "He'd have seen him if he came in."

"The man at the concert hall said the doorman hadn't seen him. When you park your car, you take the service elevator. Anyway, I know he hasn't been here." I explained about the lack of cigar ashes or butts.

I went into Victor's bedroom, Sean following at my heels,

and the room was exactly as I had last seen it. "Maybe he was in his studio!" I exclaimed, hope soaring again.

We went down the hall to the area where the wall between two bedrooms had been knocked out to form a large studio. It was tiled and insulated for soundproofing. The room was austerely simple. The white walls held no adornment except a few posters from his own and other concerts, and an embarrassing collection of Playboy centerfolds. Their airbrushed innocence appeared to interest Sean quite as much as it interested my uncle.

There was a wall of sound equipment on one side: tape recorder, amplifying equipment, speakers, a stereo radio and record player. In the middle of the room was a high stool and a music stand in front of it with a sheet of music spread out. The floor around this area was littered with discarded sheets of music. Rhoda wasn't allowed in here. There was also a desk in a corner where Victor composed his occasional pieces and did his personal correspondence.

While I looked around the room, Sean tore himself away from the centerfolds and strolled to the desk. He hastily rifled the papers on its surface. My uncle didn't smoke in this room. There wasn't even an ashtray.

"I don't come in here very often. He doesn't like to be disturbed," I said. "I don't see any sign that he's been here."

Sean began tugging at the locked drawers of the desk, which struck me as rather presumptuous. "You won't find him in there, Sean. That's his personal stuff. Love letters, bank books, whatever work he's composing. He wouldn't have been at his desk tonight."

Sean left the desk and walked back to me. "What do you want to do next?"

I put my hand on my forehead, which had developed a nagging ache and felt warm to the touch. "I don't know what to do. Eleanor Strathroy may have heard something. Maybe he phoned her about the party—to cancel it, I mean, or . . ." But I couldn't really picture Victor cancelling a party devised for his sole honor and glory when it would have given him such pleasure to attend it. The mayor was going and everything. If this were a publicity stunt, he would have cancelled the second concert.

"It's worth a try," Sean urged.

We went back to use the phone in the living room. When Eleanor, with three servants, answered her own phone, I knew she was in a state of distraction, too. Her voice was strident, querulous. If she hadn't been worried, she would have been doing her imitation of Bette Davis.

"Cassie, where are you?" was her first question.

"I'm at the apartment."

"Is he there?" she asked, almost before I finished speaking.

"No, I was hoping you'd have heard from him. He's not with you, then?"

"I haven't heard from him since ten o'clock this morning. He's had an accident," she decided dolefully. "Victor would never disappoint me like this without a good reason. Did you try the hospitals?"

"The people at Roy Thomson did. He's not in the hospital," I assured her, trying to get confidence from a vacuum.

"I can't understand what happened. He wasn't drinking today, was he?" Her voice was carefully lowered, to hide her words from listeners at her end.

"No. He wouldn't before a concert. You'll let me know right away if you hear from him? And I'll call you if he turns up here."

"Yes, of course. What a shambles! Half the party came on here and I'm trying to entertain with my head in a whirl. I wish they'd go home." There was a trace of the Bette Davis growl in her last speech. I thought that pretty soon Eleanor would find some entertainment in her role of worried and loyal mistress.

"I'm awfully sorry about the party,"

"Dear child, your mustn't apologize. It's not your fault, and not Victor's either. Something has happened to him. If only Ronald were here," she sighed, her voice petering out.

"He's not home yet?"

"Not till tomorrow. I must get back to my guests. Thanks for calling, Cassie. Bye."

I hung up and sat frowning into the receiver. I had run out of ideas of how to find Victor. As I sat thinking, Sean came out of the studio. He was frowning, too.

"Maybe it's time to call the police, Cassie," he suggested hesitantly.

"And report a missing adult, gone for all of three or four hours? They'd think I was neurotic."

His look of hesitancy deepened to doubt. "Is there any chance he got loaded somewhere? Pre-concert jitters—something like that? I read the newspapers. If you think he's tied one on, I could take a run around his favorite bars and get him home."

"He'd never get drunk in public. He's too proud and too jealous of his reputation. He'd hole up in his own digs for a binge. Besides, he was looking forward to this concert. He wasn't in a drinking mood."

"If you say so." We looked dejectedly at each other for a minute, then Sean spoke. "I don't know about Victor, but it's time you and I had a little something. Where's the liquor cabinet?"

I hate the woody, poisonous taste of Scotch, but it's part of my diplomatic training to take it without wincing, so I made two Scotch and sodas. No calories in the mix anyway. A diplomat can hardly order a piña colada. We took our drinks to the sofa to talk. I went over when I'd last seen my uncle, what his normal routine would be before a concert, and the reasons why I thought he hadn't been in the apartment, though his car parked below suggested he'd been here. I told him about the tuxedo being gone from his room when I got home from work after five. Actually I hadn't seen it since yesterday.

"I imagine a guy like Victor has a housekeeper?" he said.

"Yes, Rhoda Gardiner. She leaves at five. I'll call her and ask when she last saw him."

I know Rhoda mostly through notes, as she comes after I go to work and is gone when I get home, but I'd met her a few times and knew she was no jewel of a woman. Her chocolate cake is about the best thing about her. She told me with an utter lack of concern that Mr. Mazzini had played his violin in the morning and left the apartment sometime during the afternoon, taking his tuxedo and violin with him. She couldn't pinpoint "sometime" more closely.

"Did he seem like himself?" I asked.

"Who else would he seem like?"

"He wasn't nervous or anything?"

"He ate some salami and bread. He wasn't too nervous to eat

anyway, but he was a bit jumpy. The concert, I figured. He was in the studio all morning. Did you get my note about dinner?"

"Yes, thanks."

"That's all I can tell you." The TV was playing in the background. Rhoda had adopted the stars of the nighttime soaps for her own family. I knew she wanted to get back to them and hung up to tell Sean what she'd said.

Sean rubbed his moustache. "What do we do now?" he asked.

"We could have a look in his car and see if his tux is there," I decided. "There's a spare set of keys on a hook in the kitchen."

We got them and went down the service elevator to the parking garage. Victor drives a white Corvette. It's not really all that comfortable, but he likes the looks of it. The tux was still there in its bag, hung over the passenger seat. There was no sign of his violin. We examined the rest of the car while we were there—glove compartment, floor—but didn't discover any clues.

"He's disappeared. Just disappeared into thin air," I said, defeated. "The only thing I can think of is that somebody murdered him."

Another of my visions sprang into my head—a gruesome scene of two masked men jumping out of the shadows, hitting Victor on the head with a blackjack and dragging him into a dark alley. Except that it must have happened in broad daylight and it must have happened here, in or near this underground parking lot, as he'd never made it to the apartment. Someone must have been following him or been waiting in the garage.

"If he was here, and he wasn't upstairs, then maybe he's *still* here," Sean said logically, and began looking around the parking lot. Into cars, around and between them, even under them, but of course my uncle wasn't there. He wasn't anywhere. Logic bedamned, he'd vanished.

"Maybe he didn't drive to the Casa Loma. Maybe he took a cab," Sean suggested.

"He drove. I asked him. He drives half a block. Any excuse to get into his car. Besides, Rhoda said he left with his violin and the tuxedo. The tux is in the car, and the violin's gone. He had the violin at the Casa Loma."

"He could have parked here and taken a cab to the hall. He wouldn't need the tux for a sound check. He'd need the violin, so maybe he left the suit in the car. I wonder if the car's broken down."

Despite my aspersions on his logic, he got in and started it up. It worked just fine. I knew Victor wouldn't have taken a cab.

"I dread to think of going back to that damned empty apartment," I said, with a sudden shudder.

He put a consoling hand on my arm and gave me a bracing, tender smile. "Come on, don't get yourself psyched out. Let's think about this logically. There's got to be an explanation. He was here after five, and he had a concert at eight. Now if he was a rational man, what would he do in the three hour interval? He'd get himself something to eat, right?"

"Rhoda left supper. He didn't touch it. He wasn't in the apartment." I had a sudden jolt of inspiration. "Maybe he ate out, in a restaurant close enough that he didn't bother to drive."

"That's probably it. Where would be the likeliest spot?"

"We sometimes eat at the Four Seasons, just up the road. Let's go there and talk to the manager."

He took my arm and we left. I was suddenly very thankful for Sean's sane company. I didn't even want to think about enduring this evening alone.

We walked over to the restaurant in the hotel. It was a lovely spot, but I wasn't there to soak up glamor. The maitre d' recognized Victor Mazzini's niece. "Good evening, Ms. Newton," he smiled.

"Good evening." I asked if my uncle had been here for dinner.

"Not today," he said. He seemed a little surprised at the question. "A table for two?"

"No, thanks. We're—just going to have a drink at the bar," I said, as I felt some explanation was necessary for being in there.

We walked off toward the bar. "We're wasting our time," I said to Sean.

"We might as well check out the bar while we're here." I gave a mutinous stare but kept walking. The actual bar was populated solely by men, though there were women sitting at the tables in the lounge. We were shown to a small table and handed a list of drinks.

"You won't want to go up to the bar, with all those guys leering at you," Sean said, making it sound plausible for him to accost the bartender.

"It's a waste of time," I repeated.

"But since we're here . . ." He was already on his feet, heading for the bar.

I watched as he did his questioning. I noticed a bill being discreetly palmed by the bartender, and tried vainly to overhear the conversation. I had to interpret by their expressions— Sean's querying, alert, the bartender nodding his head first, smiling, but soon the nod became a negative shake. Yes, he knew Victor Mazzini but he hadn't seen him this evening.

"Zilch," Sean grimaced when he came back to me.

When the waiter came with our order, I decided to resume control of the investigation. "You're pretty busy here tonight," I smiled. "That's a good piano player."

"The crowd from Roy Thomson Hall—I hear the violinist didn't show," he replied.

"Victor Mazzini," I nodded. "Do you know him at all? Does he ever come here?"

"To the dining room, but no the bar. I've never seen him here." He left.

I sipped my Scotch and tried to plan a new strategy. "I think I should go back to the apartment," I said to Sean.

"You're right. This is wasting time." He gulped the last half of his drink in one swallow, and we left.

At the door to the apartment, I clutched the knob to steady the door while I inserted the key. The knob turned under my fingers, and the door opened inwards. I felt a spasm of shock followed by fear. Something told me I should be glad, that obviously my uncle was home, but I didn't believe it. I felt more frightened than before. Sean stared at the door, then at me. "I left the door locked," I whispered.

Strangely enough, he didn't show any sign of hope either, but only a tense, wary stiffening of his body, ready for action. He stepped forward, listened a minute, then kicked the door inward. There were no lights on, so he reached in and flicked the switch.

"Christ on a crutch!" he exclaimed.

I peered over his shoulder into a scene of chaos. The strewn pillows, the opened drawers, the disarranged furniture told us the apartment had been ransacked while we were out.

For one brief moment, everything went black. My head felt light, giddy. My knees suddenly turned to water. I'd never fainted in my entire life, but this shock, coming on top of a whole evening of worry, was enough to do it. Through the singing in my ears, I heard Sean's rumbling voice, and felt the reassuring pressure of his hands on my arms.

"Steady now. Let me go first."

I didn't give him an argument, but went in behind him, on shaking legs, waiting for some new calamity to befall me.

CHAPTER 3

"Was Victor a sloppy uncle, or would you say this is someone else's work?" Sean asked. It didn't strike me as the optimum moment for a joke.

"Like a pin."

I walked in, picked a gold velvet cushion up from the floor, tossed it on the sofa and took a good look around. The first impression of vandalism was unfounded, the place was only messed up. There weren't any slash marks, no sofa or chairs with their stuffing pulled out. I automatically began tidying up, and was glad to have something physical to do, while Sean made a quick tour of the apartment.

When he came back he said, "Is anything missing?"

"I don't think so."

"Maybe you ought to leave that till the police have a look around."

"I'm not calling the police." I didn't know when the decision had been made, but suddenly I said it, and knew I meant it. "Victor has a European tour lined up for early autumn. He doesn't need a scandal at this juncture. I want to find out what's going on before I call the police."

"You realize whoever got in here has a key?" he asked calmly, and waited for this news to sink in. When my face had turned white and my mouth fallen open, he continued. "Who'd have one, other than yourself and you uncle? Does this Eleanor lady have one?"

"As far as I know, she only comes when she's invited. Of course I'm away all day. It's his place—I don't ask questions."

"There's another thing to consider, Cassie. We were gone for under half an hour. Whoever did this must have been watching the place, waiting for his chance . . ."

A surge of emotion, part anger, part terror, welled up in me. "Comforting thought," I said, trying to sound as calm as he looked.

"You ought to talk to the doorman while things are still fresh in his mind."

"That sounds like a good idea," I agreed, but I felt incapable of moving. I sat down, crossed my legs and drew a deep sigh. He looked surprised. "I'm just catching my breath."

"Do you want me to go?"

"If you feel up to it."

He went out, setting the lock on the door behind him. I just sat, staring at the wall and the lap of my expensive dress till he came back.

I knew by his dour expression he hadn't learned anything. "No luck," he said. "Anybody who came into the building the last half hour either lives here or had been invited by somebody who does. Whoever came in must have used the service elevator from the parking garage."

"You need a key to get in the back door of the building as well. Sometimes the door sticks though, and doesn't lock properly. Anyway, how'd he get into the apartment?"

"Any likely suspects here in the building itself?" he asked.

I shook my head. It was ridiculous to think the neighbors— mostly well-to-do business, professional or retired people— had done this thing. We only knew them to nod to. There was a flakey redhead next door who glared every time she saw me with Victor and lifted a disbelieving brow when he introduced me as his niece. I thought there might have been something between them before I came, but I didn't look on my uncle's disappearance as a crime of passion. And if it were, I was the one who would have disappeared.

"I guess the next question is *why*," Sean said. He sat on the sofa and corrugated his forehead in my direction.

"Obviously whoever did this was looking for something," I said.

"Yeah. I wonder if he found it."

"Did you look in his studio?" Sean nodded. "Had his desk been tampered with?"

He shook his head. "Did he keep much cash in the apartment?" he asked.

It was my turn to shake my head. "There's a jewelry box on his dresser. Want to take a look at it and see if it's been rifled?"

He brought it out, but as far as I could remember, nothing was missing. There was nothing worth stealing in it. Victor bought his "jewelry" at a place that sold zircons or something that looked like diamonds. Good costume jewelry was what he wore, and counted on his reputation to endow it with the aura of authenticity.

We talked about this for a minute, then Sean took another long look around. "It's only *big* things that were disarranged. Those cupboard doors were open," he said, tossing his head towards the side wall, where cupboards about a yard high and twice as wide now stood closed. "The sofa and chairs were pulled aside, but whoever was here didn't bother to look in small drawers. Your room was hardly touched. The bottom of the bedspread had been lifted up onto the bed, and the clothes in your closet pulled aside."

"You think he was looking for something big then?" I asked. "How big?"

"Maybe something no bigger than a violin."

"We can eliminate elephants and grand pianos then. Sean, his violin isn't in his car!"

"I suppose it was worth a lot of money. You mentioned it was a Guan—something or other."

"A Guarneri. It's worth quite a bit—maybe he *did* drop it off here. He had it at the Casa Loma."

"Now will you call the police?" he asked hopefully.

How could I tell him what I really believed—that Victor was pulling off a cheap publicity stunt? Sean obviously thought I was either heartless or deranged, but I stuck to my guns, making much of the harm a scandal would do his career. If the police were called in, the whole thing would be blown up in the papers, and his European tour could be cancelled. There was bound to be some talk after tonight's cancellation, but if he showed up by tomorrow, it might be contained to a minor scandal.

I puzzled over Victor's itinerary after he left the Casa Loma, trying to figure out why he'd brought the car back, but in my own mind, the missing violin convinced me that he was hiding somewhere in a room, practicing away for tomorrow night. A car was a big thing to hide, and the plates were traceable, so he'd left it here. What I couldn't understand was why he'd come home and messed up the apartment. Was it to cause some suggestion that he'd been abducted? Did Victor *want* me to call the police? I noticed he'd been careful not to harm his good paintings. The Alex Colville, his pride and joy, hung unmarred, and it was worth several thousand dollars. Or maybe he came back for his special imported cigars. He was a real addict.

I took Victor's jewelry box back to his room as an excuse to check the cigars. His humidor, a dark mahogany box that looked like a coffin for a hamster, all lined and insulated, was open and empty. I had been at the door Monday evening, talking to him when he filled it. That supply ought to have lasted at least a week. My heart lifted with relief just before it hardened with anger at his trick.

What a lot of bother he'd caused! Scared me out of my wits, left the concert goers without their concert, the Roy Thomson manager in a fury, and Eleanor with about fifty pounds of lobster that would be thrown out. But that was Victor all over. Spoiled rotten, a selfish, senile delinquent. He should be turned over somebody's knee and walloped. And on top of it all, I now had to go out and politely get rid of Sean Bradley, who'd been so helpful all night.

Sean noticed my relieved expression as soon as I went back to the living room. I could tell by the curious light in his eyes that he knew something had happened in the bedroom and scanned my brain for an explanation that would satisfy him.

"What is it? What did you find?" he asked eagerly.

No clever inspiration came to me. "Nothing," I said, trying to sound nonchalant. "I've just been thinking about it, and I'm sure he's all right. That's all."

"Were you praying?" His voice rose in disbelief on the last word. "You look so—serene."

I grasped at this straw. "Yes, I was." My sober mien dared him to question it, or laugh. He just went on looking. For a minute, I thought a smile was going to break, but I held my own mouth steady as a ruler and stared him down.

He cleared his throat, looked away once or twice, then screwed up his courage to speak. "I'm not knocking your religion, Cassie, but I still think you ought to get some—uh—worldly help. The Lord helps those who help themselves," he added with a sideways look to see the effect of this platitude.

"In that case, Victor should be fine," I said grimly.

His lips clamped shut, and when he spoke a minute later, he sounded offended. "I was just trying to help. I take it you don't plan to let me in on whatever you found in there. I was hoping we could work on this together, but if you want to go it alone, that's your privilege." He got up and walked stiffly toward the door.

I remembered a saying of Samuel Johnson's that there are people we would like very well to drop, but wouldn't want to be dropped by. Sean was like that. There was a quality of genuineness in his simplicity that made it important for him to like you. You knew instinctively he wouldn't like inferior people—phonies. He'd hate Ronald Strathroy. It had something to do with troublesome morality. I knew I was going to stop him.

He was a nice, kind man. He hadn't been a bit mad when the concert was cancelled, and he'd done everything he could to help me since that time. Even bribed the bartender at the hotel. When my head was in a whirl, he'd asked all the right questions for me. I took a step after him. "Wait!" He turned back with a light of hopeful interest in his brown eyes.

"Sean, I'm sorry," I said, and took a step after him. "The thing is, Victor's an awful publicity hound. Remember I told you about the capriccio? Maybe that wasn't the surprise. I think he's just hiding out to get publicity and pep up the sale of tickets." Sean looked doubtful, and I explained in a little more detail about the sagging ticket sales.

"Wouldn't he have let *you* in on the secret?"

"Not necessarily. He's really very self-centered. Artists are like that. I haven't even thanked you for everything. I'll—I'll call you tomorrow. I'm sure he'll be home by then."

"What makes you think so?" he asked. "It doesn't add up to me. I can't see a guy coming in and mussing up his own apartment. We decided your break-in artist was looking for something, remember? More likely you'll get a phone call from the kidnapper. If you're as smart as I take you for, Cassie, you'll call the police. It's up to you, but the longer you wait, the colder the trail gets."

"Kidnapper!"

"When rich people suddenly disappear, it's usually kidnapping. I was hoping they'd just kidnapped his violin, but it's been a few hours now, and there's still no sign of Victor. Think about it." He gave me a long, dark look, and went out. Before the door clicked, he stuck his head back in and said, "Lock this after me, and put on the chain. Whoever was watching earlier is likely still out there."

On this comforting speech, he left. I ran to the door and did as he suggested. Was Sean right? Was Victor kidnapped? What could Sean possibly know? He'd never even met Victor in his life. And he didn't know the cigars were gone—I'd forgotten to tell him that. Nobody but Victor would have taken them. A kidnapper didn't take such pains for his victim's comfort. Of course it was Victor himself, the wretch, and when he came back, I'd give him the tongue lashing of his life. No wonder his wife left him!

Sleep was obviously impossible under these harrowing conditions, so I went to the sofa to think. When no new thoughts had occurred to me by ten o'clock, I turned on the TV to watch the news, and see how much coverage Victor got. He'd be annoyed that a royal visit took precedence as an opener, but he was the second feature. I listened sharply as the announcer outlined the story.

Victor Mazzini, the celebrated violinist, had failed to appear for a scheduled concert at Roy Thomson Hall. His whereabouts were unknown, but foul play was not indicated. There was a snide mention of his former fight with alchoholism. Poor Victor, he'd done himself more harm than good with this gambit. Maybe he'd meant me to call the police and show them the messed up apartment. The police weren't dopes. They'd see the lock hadn't been tampered with, and soon suspect the truth. The best thing was to sit tight and wait for him to phone or come home. He wouldn't stay away long once those old alcohol rumors resurfaced.

The next item on the news was a report on the St. Jean Baptiste celebration in Quebec. That French province has a unique provincial holiday not shared by the rest of the country. All businesses were closed; there were street parades, a picnic on top of Mount Royal in Montreal, but no demonstrations by the Separatists this year. I remembered that Ronald was in Montreal. Funny he'd gone on St. Jean Baptiste day, when the banks and brokerage houses would be closed. Or maybe he'd chosen this day on purpose. Everything would be quiet in the offices, so the meeting wouldn't be interrupted by the crush of ordinary business. I thought there might even be a measure of secrecy to his trip. Lots of businesses had left Quebec, and if Ronald was luring another one to Toronto, he wouldn't want any publicity before the fact. The Quebec government occasionally made noises about putting a stop to those business emigrations.

Eleanor phoned again before I went to bed. There was a wild flare of excitement, thinking it was Victor calling, but Eleanor's voice brought me to earth with a thump.

"Is there still no word from him?" she asked.

I considered telling her about the cigars and my suspicion, but decided against it. Eleanor wasn't a serious lady love, only a convenient companion who opened pleasant doors. I did try to console her though.

"I'm sure he'll be back tomorrow. Why don't you go to bed and try to get some sleep?" I suggested.

"Bed? I have a hundred people here. Why don't you come on over and join the party? It would be better than sitting by the phone alone," Eleanor countered.

The very mention of a party made me realize how exhausted I was. The emotional strain had drained me. "I want to be here in case he calls or comes home."

A deep sigh was transmitted along the wire. "Be sure to call me the *instant* you hear from him. No matter what the hour. I won't be sleeping in any case."

"I'll call. Goodnight, Eleanor."

I got ready for bed with no horrendous fit of nerves, but only a tense, waiting feeling that at any moment he'd come back. He *had* to come back. Sean couldn't possibly be right, that I'd get a call from kidnappers. That was ridiculous. Who'd kidnap Victor? He wasn't that rich. His life savings were pretty well tied up in this condo and a summer place he'd bought up north of Toronto. Unless they hoped to tap Eleanor for a million or so . . . In which case I feared the kidnappers were out of luck. Eleanor only spent money on herself, as far as I could see. Even tonight's party was more for herself than my uncle. He was an excuse, no more. If Victor hadn't been the guest of honor, it would have been some tenor or writer. She dabbled in the artists.

One hour, one glass of warm milk and five hundred calories of choc. cake later, I slept.

CHAPTER 4

At eight a.m., the alarm clock whirred into sound, dragging me from a deep, troubled sleep. My hand automatically went out to silence it. I was sitting up, muttering imprecations against the necessity of working for a living when a remembrance of the past night washed over me. I jumped out of bed to see if Victor had returned, but when I got to the door and saw the chain on it, I realized he couldn't have gotten in without waking me.

I padded barefoot to the kitchen, put on water for coffee and went to the shower. Twenty minutes later I sat at the table dressed in my guide's uniform and sipping coffee, debating the pros and cons of going to work today. Surely they wouldn't expect me to work. Of course I had to stay home, but I didn't want Rhoda Gardiner underfoot all day, vacuuming and rearranging the dust.

Two phone calls later I had arranged a day off for the housekeeper and myself, and I went to the door to retrieve the morning papers. Victor took all three of them. The sedate businessman's paper didn't have him on page one. The less sedate *Toronto Star* did, but without a picture—the pictures were on the Entertainment page. It was the popular rag that ran the shock-type story, hinting at my uncle's libationary past. They resurrected a photo of him with a champagne glass in his hand, wearing his wide smile. In non-libelous phrases, they left the impression he was off on a toot. At least he'd be easily recognized if he ventured out of his hiding hole.

When the intercom buzzed, I answered to the cultured accents of Ronald Strathroy. He has a voice like Devonshire cream, smooth and rich. I didn't know whether I was glad or sorry, but I wasn't surprised. Ronald could always be counted on to do the polite thing. He'd be here, with his well-tailored shoulder to lean on, but I better not sully it with a tear.

Within minutes, he was at the door. He came in like a well-oiled machine, every move a glide. Ronald was probably the smoothest man I'd ever met, and the classiest. Maybe it was the echo of an upper crust English accent that caused that impression. He'd only spent two years at Oxford, but he'd managed to assimilate the manner. When I first commented on it, he'd explained his schooling: Upper Canada College, for the sons of the elite, followed by the University of Toronto and the two years at Oxford.

His hair was the color of straw and the texture of silk. He wore it neatly barbered, a little longer than Sean. Sharp, intelligent green eyes were set in a narrow, chiselled face with a handsomely prominent nose and a crooked mouth that robbed him of dignity. His summer working outfit was a striped seersucker suit, a blue shirt and silk tie. He carried his long, lean frame as straight as a whip.

"Cassie, I've just come from home. Mom told me all about it. How ghastly for you! Have you heard from him?" he asked, placing his long-fingered hands on my upper arms. A heavy, crested ring with a bloodstone glowed on one finger. It was his father's university ring.

"Ronald, I didn't think you be back so soon. No, I haven't heard a thing."

A crease formed between his eyes. "I took an early flight this morning. I wish I'd been here with you. What on earth can have happened?"

"You couldn't have done anything. I was here; your mother was here. He just vanished," I said, hunching my shoulders in confusion. "Do you want some coffee? It's still hot."

"I should be getting to work, but okay, I'll have a cup first. I've got a million things to do at the office. Important meetings after the trip to Montreal yesterday, you know."

"How did it go?" He followed me to the kitchen, and I poured his coffee.

After we were seated, he said, "Fine, it was a success." He glanced at the newspapers on the table. I could see him trying to hide his disgust at such vulgar publicity. The mention of my being Victor Mazzini's niece might be dropped from my customary introduction. More likely, I'd be dropped altogether as soon as etiquette permitted.

"I was surprised to see on TV last night it was a holiday in Quebec. What did you do, have private meetings?" I asked.

"Yes, we met at the home of the manager of the trust company actually. A lovely mansion in Westmount—you must be familiar with the area, from being at McGill. It's all very hush-hush. We don't want the Separatists raising an uproar in parliament. That's why we chose St. Jean Baptiste day," he explained.

"Smart. I thought that was probably it."

His eyes had shifted to the newspapers again, and he read silently for a moment. "Victor should sue these people," he said and shoved the papers aside in disgust. "You don't think there's any truth in it, do you? Had he been drinking lately?"

"Just wine with dinner, nothing serious."

"Mom didn't think so either. What did the police have to say?"

"I didn't call them. Do you think I should?" I was becoming more worried the longer Victor stayed away.

"They obviously know already," he said, pointing to the papers. "They were in the parking garage downstairs when I came up. I imagine you'll be hearing from them any minute now."

I was wrenching my hands, and moved them to my lap, out of sight. "I hardly know what to tell them."

He looked surprised. "Tell them the truth," he said simply. "Answer whatever questions they ask. It obviously has nothing to do with *you*. You don't have to worry."

"It's not myself I'm worried about!" Ronald could be a mountain of selfishness at times, and he apparently thought I was as bad.

We talked for a few minutes. I told him about last night. For some reason, I didn't mention Sean Bradley. Ronald promised to be in touch, and started to leave. At the doorway, he paused and placed a light kiss on my cheek and patted my shoulder.

"He'll turn up," he said, smiling reassurance. "You know Victor—always some rig running. Mom nearly killed me when I said it, but I bet he's just hiding to create a sensation. What do you think?" A conspiratorial spark glinted in his green eyes. They were light green, more like a peridot than an emerald.

At such times, I wondered why I didn't love Ronald Strathroy. He had everything: looks, some charm, money galore, and I could probably joke him out of that air of stuffiness. Not that the word "love" had ever arisen between us, but you can't help wondering. I couldn't help wondering about his selfishness though. That's innate, not something that can be talked or joked away.

"I think you might be right," I admitted, and on an impulse, told him about the missing cigars, which I had omitted from the earlier recital of the apartment search.

"The old son-of-a-gun!" he laughed. "It's a trick for sure. He's probably hiding out at the cottage. Too bad there isn't a phone there. I have to dash. See you tonight?" The question slid out very naturally, as though we were steady companions. Dates with Ronald were usually grand affairs, arranged with much pomp and some circumstance, the circumstance usually being that Victor was along with Eleanor.

"Give me a call. I'm leaving the night open. Anything could happen."

Ronald was a little surprised at my lack of enthusiasm, but he left in good humor. Was it at all possible a romantic nature lurked beneath Ronald's silk hair? Did he feel some urge to help a damsel in distress—or had Eleanor sent him? He would have stayed around and helped me with the police if he'd been a real romantic. What was taking them so long to come hammering on the door?

I didn't forget Sean during that morning. A thought of his warm brown eyes was often with me, but unless he came to the door, I couldn't be seeing him again. Victor's phone was unlisted, and anyway tourists don't stay in town forever. I wanted to phone him, but didn't even know what hotel he was at. On a guess, I thought probably not the Hilton or King Edward, certainly not one of the small, exclusive places. But it would be downtown. The Delta Inn was a possibility—the

Royal York, tops. While I idly pondered this riddle, the phone rang. It was Sean. For no discernable reason, I felt happy.

"How'd you get my number? It's unlisted."

"It's on the phone in the apartment. I memorized it last night."

"You're quick!"

"Persistent, too. If you hadn't answered the phone, I meant to take a run over to Bloor Street. Any news?"

"He hasn't turned up. Don't say I told you so. I haven't had a call for ransom either."

"Good. What are you doing today?" he asked.

"Waiting by the phone with coffee—literally. When do you leave town?"

"Not till I've seen you again. You got a spare cup of that coffee?"

"Sure. I'll even spring for a fresh pot, if you want to waste your annual vacation sitting by a phone," I tempted.

"I'll be right over."

I was sitting with the receiver in my hand, listening to the buzz and smiling like an idiot when the police finally came to the door. They had sent a plainclothes detective named Fred Marven to interview me. He was fiftyish, overweight, flushed, and a good candidate for a heart attack. He looked around the place, asked all the obvious questions about when I had last seen my uncle, his state of mind, was there anything unusual, what was he wearing, and had I heard anything from him since last night.

I answered everything truthfully. He didn't happen to enquire whether the apartment had been broken into, and I didn't volunteer the information. I did the best job I could of acting disturbed, which wasn't too hard when I was half deranged, and concealing evidence didn't do anything to calm my nerves.

Ronald had said there were "some policemen" in the garage. The others were probably looking at the car, maybe dusting it for prints or something. I noticed Marven didn't leave the building when he left the apartment, but went down the hall to query the neighbors. It was Betty Friske's door he went to first—she's the flakey redhead who hates me. I have a strong suspicion my arrival interfered with a romance between Victor and her. Was it possible he was there, right next door all this time? How easy for him to have slipped in here after he heard Sean and me leave last night! Sean had thought someone was watching, but he never thought he was watching from such a close vantage point.

I left the door open a crack and listened. Marven didn't go into Betty's apartment. I couldn't hear his questions, but her answers came fluting down the hall quite clearly. Mostly she kept saying "No!", loud and clear. Once I overheard her say "hardly know him". That was a lie, and maybe those "No's" were also lies. I'd drop in on Betty Friske soon.

As soon as the detective got into the elevator, I went rapping on Mrs. Friske's door. She's a divorcee, somewhere in her late thirties, and still attractive in a full-blown way. She should be; as far as I can tell, she spends all her time going to beauty parlors and shopping. The only people who call at her door are delivery men. She lives expensively and drives a Porsche.

She already looked annoyed when she came to the door swathed in a Japanese geisha girl's kimono with her red curls tousled picturesquely. I realized I should have taken time to rehearse my approach to her. Caught unprepared, I blurted out, "I've got to see Victor."

She stuck a cigarette in her mouth and inhaled before answering. Through the cloud of smoke, her sharp gray eyes gimleted into me. "Welcome to the club, Miss Mazzini," she said grimly.

"My name's Newton. Cassie Newton."

She cocked a penciled brow at me. "Niece, I thought he said."

"On my mother's side. Mom's his sister."

"Sure," she said, chewing back a smile at my cute guide's uniform. "I have no idea where he is. I already told the police."

I looked over her shoulder, wondering how I could talk my way into her apartment to look for clues. She started closing the door. I could see a slice of a lovely living room in there all done up in flowing Art Deco, with furniture that belonged in a Fred Astaire movie or a bar. She must be getting some fantastic alimony. There was a hard-edged finish to Betty that said she wasn't born to this lavish life.

"If he turns up, let me know," she said. "We have unfinished business, Victor and me. And he better turn up, or he'll be sorry. So far I haven't told the police anything. So far," she repeated, with a very meaningful lift of her brows. She had a weird purplish-pink eye shadow on. Her eyes looked bruised.

"Thank you," I said, as the door closed firmly in front of me. I was sorry I'd bothered going—I didn't need that implicit threat to make my day. What criminal business could my uncle be engaged in with that tart? But at any rate, I was convinced Victor wasn't hiding out there. Or if he was, Betty Friske was a consummate actress.

Before Sean came, I changed out of my uniform. It wasn't particularly flattering, and if we went out, I didn't want to wear it on the streets. I put on a cotton dress, navy with big white polka dots. The fresh coffee was filtered by the time Sean came.

He was back in his tourist clothes; the jeans, boots, a checked shirt, jeans jacket tossed over his shoulder like a lasso, and the Western hat in his hand. All set to go herding cattle along Bloor Street.

"Where'd you tether Trigger?" I asked.

"My wheels are downstairs."

I felt mean, jibing at a man too innocent to even recognize sarcasm, let alone retaliate. "The police just left," I told him.

"Good, I'm glad you called them. What did they have to say?" he asked eagerly.

I filled him in while we sat by the phone, having our coffee. During the next half hour, nobody called except Eleanor, and she had nothing to say except that the party went fine, just fine, and I mustn't worry about anything. I told her the police had been here, and she thought it *infra-dig* of me to have spoken to them, I believe. "That was encroaching of them," she exclaimed.

"Ronald is so worried about you," she said a little later, to my surprised gratification. I rang off as soon as politely possible and relayed the conversation to Sean, especially the part about Ron being worried.

He soon got tired of sitting and asked what we were going to do about finding my uncle. "He must have friends, some place he'd go to if he just went off for the hell of it. That's what you still think, isn't it?" he demanded, piercing me with a sharp eye.

"It's a possibility."

"I read the papers this morning. 'No foul play indicated,' they said. What I haven't figured out is how you knew it last night in his bedroom. What did I miss? I didn't see any bottles, didn't smell booze. You went in there looking like a candidate for the Spanish Inquisition, and came out looking as if you'd beaten the rap."

Despite the anachronism, he was too sharp to bluff, so I broke down and told him about the cigars being gone.

"Are you sure they were there when you left for the concert?"

"Pretty sure. And I'm positive his humidor wasn't open. I noticed it, looking like a little coffin."

He measured me, trying to decide whether to take offence. "Why didn't you tell me about that last night? In fact, you were pretty reluctant to tell me anything."

"I didn't want to spread it around that he's hiding—it looks bad. People might get the idea he was drunk, and I don't believe that."

"I see. And naturally I, a tourist in town, would've grabbed the closest phone and announced it to the papers. What do you take me for?"

"A stranger. Who knows what a stranger might do? Anyway, I did tell you."

"Eventually. I don't know what your average run-of-the-mill stranger might do, but this one is getting damned bored doing nothing. Have you come up with any ideas as to where he might be?"

I thought about it for a minute. "He has a cottage up north. Not too far—about forty miles. There's no phone, or I'd give him a call. Or we could drive up . . ."

He was already on his feet, reaching for his hat. "We could be there in an hour. You won't miss much here. If he comes back, he'll be here waiting for you."

"All right. Let's go." You can only look at a mute phone so long without picking it up and throwing it out a window. It was a lovely day, and it was a nice drive up to Victor's cottage in the Caledon Hills. Maybe he *was* there; he didn't seem to be anywhere else.

Mrs. Friske's door opened a crack when we went into the hall. I wondered if she always monitored the traffic so closely, or was on the alert today for my uncle's return. Whatever was going on between her and Victor, I hoped she'd keep it from the police for a little longer.

"Friend of yours?" Sean asked, after she'd closed the door. He didn't miss much.

"Not particularly. Why, were you hoping for an introduction?"

"I didn't get that good a look at her. If she always haunts the hall like she is now, she might be able to tell us something."

"I already asked. No luck." I didn't add her worrying message to Victor. There are some skeletons best kept in the closet, and I was worried about just what kind of bones I was dealing with here. Did women still prosecute for breach of promise? I couldn't imagine what else but romance Betty and Victor shared. Whatever her intentions might have been, I doubted very much he'd used the word "marriage". He was too experienced for that. And so was she.

CHAPTER 5

Sean was still driving the same rented car, a silver Monte Carlo. I gave him directions, and we were soon past the builtup commercial area and suburbs, heading north.

A beatific smile took strong possession of Sean's face. "God's country," he crooned. "Jeez, would I love to live somewhere like this. No pollution, no traffic."

"No restaurants, no stores, no people to talk to. Just a man and his hoss."

"And his woman," he added, flashing a smile.

I could see what he meant though. The sky was as blue and smiling as Irish eyes. A frolicsome wind blew a few cotton clouds along, high overhead. The world out here looked brand new. The leaves were still shiny, a pale shade of green. Solemn pines stood guard over the countryside. Lazy holsteins grazing in meadows lent the wholesomely contrived look of calendar art. It wasn't the right place to worry about kidnapping. It was a place for a picnic or falling in love. Or in Sean's case, a place to fish.

"There must be some lively fishing here."

"That's a contradiction in terms. Besides, don't you need water to fish?" Water was missing from the landscape.

"Yeah." A minute later he said, "What's Victor like?"

"He's Italian, with all the stereotypical qualities. Passionate, volatile, fun-loving, artistic, talented. He's also selfish, ego-centric, vain—well, he's a man after all," I added blandly. I could feel Sean's head turn toward me, and I looked out the window, unconcerned.

"He doesn't worry much about tomorrow, as long as he's enjoying himself today," I continued. "Of course I didn't know him very well before this summer. He used to visit us about once a year. It was a grand occasion. Mom cooked for two days before he came, and we all talked about it for a week after, then forgot him till the next visit. He used to bring us all presents," I said, remembering those visits with pleasure.

"Who's us all?"

"Mom and Dad, Ricky and me. Rick's my brother."

"Older or younger?"

"Younger. He's seventeen."

"That's what I thought. I had you pegged for an only child, till you mentioned that 'all' a couple of times."

"I can see you're dying to explain your brilliance. Okay, what made you think I was an only child?"

"You're cocksure, aggressive. Me, I'm the middle kid," he said, pleading for sympathy from the corner of his eye.

I gave an ironic laugh. "And only son. You like to take charge, too."

"I thought I was being downright agreeable! Didn't fool you, huh? Well you're right about the sisters. I know all about women, except what they do for fourteen hours at a time in the bathroom. Come out looking worse than when they went in. Hair all frizzed, too much makeup, smelling like French— uh—waitresses. I notice you don't use much makeup."

I suppose in Nebraska that might have been called a compliment. "You won't smell my particular bouquet on many waitresses. It's real French perfume. Victor gave it to me. An ounce would cost me a week's salary. Of course he only gave me a tenth of an ounce."

"You haven't let me get close enough to smell it," he ventured. There was a lupine quality in his eyes again.

"That Old Spice you showered in would cover the smell. Good perfume is subtle."

"Yeah," he grunted. A minute later he grunted again. "Real pretty country. What's a Yankee like you doing up here?"

I told him about my studies, and my plan to be a diplomat. It's a subject on which I easily get carried away. Somehow he arrived at the truth: what I really wanted was a sinecure that allowed me to loll in the lap of luxury, while performing ostensible duties of a highly cerebral but physically undemanding sort.

"What you want's a rich husband," he concluded.

"Don't be silly. I could have that, if that's all I wanted!" I objected, and elevated Ronald to red-hot pursuer. Damned hardware salesman. What did he know about anything? "Ronald Strathroy—he's the son of Eleanor, the lady that's always calling," I said. "I pointed her out last night at the hall."

"How come Ronald doesn't phone himself?"

"He comes in person," I retaliated. "He came this morning, just before you called. In fact, it was Ronald who mentioned that Victor was probably at his cottage."

"Doesn't Ronald care for music? How come he didn't go with you to the concert last night?"

"He was in Montreal on business. The Strathroys own a brokerage house. They're taking over a Montreal trust company, but it's very hush-hush."

"I won't phone that one in to the newspapers either then."

We drove on a while in silence; not a comfortable silence, but an edgy one. After about a mile, Sean got over his pique and spoke. Having failed to spot water, he said, "Must be good hunting in those woods."

"I wouldn't know. I don't believe in killing innocent, helpless animals to eat," I answered grandly.

"Vegetarian, are you?"

Being caught in a tight corner, I hastily reviewed our past acquaintance and remembered I hadn't eaten any meat in his presence. "Of course."

"Do you know where the musk for that expensive perfume you're dowsed in comes from?" he asked.

"I don't want to know! I wear leather shoes, and I know where leather comes from. That doesn't mean I approve of senseless killing of helpless animals. Furthermore, one doesn't dowse herself in French perfume. It's dabbed on. Let's talk about something less gross."

"Tell me something," Sean said, without removing his eyes from the road. "Are we having a fight?"

"No, Sean," I told him sweetly. "When we're having a fight, you won't have to ask."

He gave a begrudging chuckle that started in the pit of his stomach and rumbled up his chest, out his lips. "Do you fight with Ronald?" he asked.

"Certainly not. Ronald is a gentleman. He always does what I want." Talk about a whopper! Ronald was the epitome of selfishness.

"Sounds like a wimp to me. You won't forget to tell me when I have to make a turn, will you? That's a question, not a command."

We were soon climbing a county road that curved between high rock cliffs, with modern homes perched precariously here and there. Victor's was one of them, reached by a road that wheeled around the rear of the rocks. Some of the occupants lived here year round, which necessitated a good road.

Victor hadn't had the cottage built himself, but picked it up at a bargain price at an estate sale. Victor wouldn't have chosen a modern slab of cedar with walls of glass, but I noticed that despite his alleged love of old things, Sean was enamored of the place. Mostly he loved the site and the view, I thought. He took a long, appreciative look around, inhaled the fresh spring aroma of new grass and pines before we went to the door. We had already observed, of course, that there was no car parked outside and no lights on within.

"This was dumb. Really dumb," I said. "Victor couldn't be here, or his car would be gone from the parking garage."

"He'd have hired a car," Sean countered. "But if he did, I don't see any sign of it. Let's go in."

"More dumbness. We didn't bring the keys!"

"You forgot the key?" he asked, delighted at my lapse.

"I hope you enjoyed the drive. That's all we're going to get out of this venture."

"Hold your horses. I'll be right back." He went to the car, and came back carrying a small piece of hardware from the glove compartment.

While he pried the rear door open, very easily, and with no appreciable damage, I wondered if all hired cars came supplied with this criminal piece of hardware. "Lucky that was in the glove compartment," I said, making no effort to hide my suspicion.

"Lucky? I put it there. I thought you might forget the key. I'm a hardware man, remember? Your uncle should install dead bolts," he said, while he finished his breaking and entering job.

There was nothing remarkable to note in the kitchen. The cedar cabinet doors were ajar—that's all. Sean went to the cupboard and pointed out that the doors had magnets to hold them shut. "Funny they were all hanging open," he said.

He lifted up a few cans. "Victor doesn't share your vegetarian taste. Tinned ham, salmon, chicken soup."

I ignored his taunt. "Nobody's been here. There's no sign of eating or dirty dishes."

We went into the living room that stretched along the front of the cottage, with a glass front giving a breathtaking view of treetops and patchwork-quilt farms in the valley below. No damage had been done here, nothing was taken, but things were awry. Not quite helter-skelter, but the furniture was out of place. A pine chest against one wall had been opened and not closed. Victor and I had been here on the May 24th weekend, a long weekend in Canada, to celebrate the Queen's birthday. We hadn't been back since, and we hadn't left it like this.

"Let's have a gander at the bedrooms," Sean suggested.

The three bedrooms were all in a row at the rear of the cottage. They were slightly disarranged too. The closet doors hung open, the bedspreads had been pulled up onto the beds, as though someone had lifted them to look beneath and not bothered to return them. Some boxes had been taken down from the high closet shelves and placed on the floor.

"No damage, just a quick search," he said. His voice was flat, not surprised.

I looked around at the boxes and dressers. "Someone was here all right, but I don't see anything missing."

We wandered back to the living room. The expensive hifi equipment, the TV, the binoculars—all the things a thief would have taken were still in place.

"What do you make of it?" I asked him, as I didn't know what to make of it myself. "The locks weren't tampered with.

It must have been Victor himself. Oh I know *you* got in without any trouble, but not everybody's a hardware expert."

"Face it, Cassie, whoever was here and in the apartment too was looking for something—something he thought was hidden. If it had been your uncle, he'd have known where he put the thing, wouldn't he?"

"Yes, I guess he would." I walked all around the room, looking for clues. In movies, the crook is kind enough to leave behind a match flap, a handkerchief with an initial, a cuff link or a cigarette butt. The shiny ashtrays were unmarred by a single ash. There was none of that repulsive lingering odor of stale cigar smoke either, which was pretty good confirmation that Victor hadn't been here. Or Betty Friske, for that matter. She chain smoked cigarettes. It would have taken several minutes to search the place. I'd never seen her without a cigarette, even on the elevator.

"Could you break into my apartment with that little gizmo you used to get in here?" I asked. This unsettling thought sent a little shiver up my spine.

"No, not with that dead bolt. Whoever got in there had the key for sure."

"Well, only Victor had the key, as far as I know."

"Yeah, *had*. Maybe the breaker-in got it from him," he suggested, turning my shiver into a full-fledged shudder.

After the first gulp of fright, I returned to my senses. "He must be a very friendly sort of kidnapper, if you're back on that track. What he actually took was Victor's cigars."

"You don't know that. Maybe there was something else in that humidor. But it's not big enough . . ."

"No, he'd have searched the apartment first. The very fact that someone has been here makes it pretty clear he didn't find what he was after at the apartment. But what did you mean—it's not big enough? The humidor is big enough for money or jewels or an important paper."

Sean was flushing uneasily. Why? "What I mean is," he explained, "we kind of thought it was a bigger thing the guy was looking for. You remember we talked about it last night. Little places weren't searched. It was under beds, in closets, behind sofas that he looked, in both cases. The canisters in the kitchen, for instance—he didn't touch them. I don't know whether you noticed, but the small drawers weren't opened either. The desk drawers were all neatly closed."

"You still think it was his violin they were after? Victor had it with him at the Casa Loma. If that's all the man wanted, he'd have got it when he got my uncle. He wouldn't still be searching for it."

I was looking around the room as we had this discussion. It was then it first occurred to me that Sean was very sharp to have noticed the size of places that had been searched. It might have occurred to me eventually, but he came out with it not a minute after we saw the state of the apartment the night before. Almost as if he knew the violin was what the man was after, or as if he'd been trained in this kind of work.

I turned and examined him while he looked around. He looked kind of ragged around the edges for a policeman. A private detective, possibly? "Are you some kind of cop?" I asked.

His reaction struck me as overdone. "Me?" he asked, his eyes stretched wide, forehead crinkled like a washboard. "I'm a hardware salesman. Plains of Nebraska, remember?"

"Where in Nebraska?" If he said Omaha, which was the only city I could think of, I'd give my suspicions more thought.

"North Platte," he said, without a second's hesitation.

"Where's that?"

"In the southwest, on the Platte River. You must have heard of North Platte!" he said. His injured accent sounded very genuine.

"Sure, I've heard of it." But I'd get out the atlas as soon as I got home and check its location all the same. And I still found it fishy that he'd memorized the apartment phone number, too, in the midst of the confusion last night.

"What made you think I was a cop?" he asked, deciding to be flattered at the imputation. At least I hadn't accused him of being on the other side of the law. That possibility hadn't occurred to me at the time. That came quite a bit later.

"You pick up on things so quickly."

As I studied his face, a smile peeped out, showing his overlapped teeth. "I love this kind of stuff," he admitted sheepishly. "I watch all the detective shows on TV. Read MacDonald, Hammett, Chandler. It's a real treat for me, being able to horn in on this case. I even thought of being a private eye, but there wasn't much call for it in North Platte."

"I know how you feel. There isn't much opportunity to be a Sybarite in Maine. I kind of enjoy mysteries myself, but I wish somebody other than Victor were involved in this one. Well, what would Philip Marlowe do next? Bash somebody on the head, I expect."

"It's old Phil who gets bashed around. Our best bet is to get back to the apartment. There's not much to be done here. Somebody came and looked around. I wonder if he got what he was looking for," he added, rubbing his chin.

"If the apartment has been ransacked again, we'll know he didn't find what he was after here."

It was time to give some serious consideration to the possibility Victor hadn't kidnapped himself. This wasn't one of his publicity stunts. I had been quite sure we'd find him here, playing his own records or his violin. My nose had been ready for the assault of stale cigar smoke; I even found myself missing it. I was lonesome for Victor and worried sick. "Let's go," I said. My voice was husky.

"I've scared you with my talk of break-ins and kidnapping. There's one reassuring thing in it," he pointed out. He put his hands on my arms, just the way Ronald had that morning, but his hands felt kinder, warmer. His nails, I noticed, were cut off flat and short with scissors. He had a half moon scar on his right knuckle. A hammer would make a little mark like that. Ronald's nails were manicured.

"The cigars," he said, "that looks as if he's alive all right. And whoever's got him, they're bighearted enough to care for his comfort. He can't be tied up either, or he wouldn't be able to smoke them. He's just being kept locked up somewhere till the guy gets what he's after."

"But what *is* he after? And maybe the man took the cigars for himself. Maybe he smokes, too." I looked up from Sean's hands to his eyes, grave with sympathy. "None of it makes any sense. Victor had his violin with him, so that's not what they're looking for. He doesn't own a fortune—a violinst doesn't make as much money as you might think. He has alimony payments, and between this cottage and his apartment in Toronto, he doesn't have a bulging bank account."

Sean heard me out patiently. About midway through my speech, he dropped his hands. "I don't know, but whoever's got him sure as hell isn't keeping him locked up for no reason. He must have something that's pretty valuable."

"His talent is his most valuable possession, and no one can steal that."

I cudgelled my brain all the way home, hardly noticing the stunning scenery. What did Victor have that was worth stealing? The capriccio he'd written for me (maybe for me)? That wasn't very likely. He wasn't much of a composer. And if he'd meant to perform it in public, he'd have copyrighted it first. He wasn't a rank amateur. He travelled internationally, which drew forth the specter of spying. A formula, a microdot film? No, thieves wouldn't look under beds for that. Some sort of new computer secret in the form of software? When I suggested this to Sean, he gave a disbelieving stare.

"I think we can rule out international espionage," he said very firmly.

Hunger pangs assailed me as we drove home. I could hear Sean's stomach complaining, too, and looked hopefully at the McDonald's signs. I was already salivating and totalling up the calories in a Big Mac and fries. He noticed the second time I craned my neck around to gaze longingly at the golden arches.

"Keep your eyes peeled for a health food joint," he said. "I could go for a Big Mac right about now myself." It must have been ESP.

I could hardly remember how I'd talked myself into this vegetarian corner. Oh yes, it was his comment about hunting.

"Don't let me keep you from eating. I can have some fries and a milk shake." But it was a cheeseburger I craved, with the cheese melting in an orange river over the beef.

Sean pulled in at the next McDonald's, and proved to be a perfect gentleman after all. He brought me a Big Mac, and insisted I eat it, just this once. "You need protein to keep up your strength," he ordered quite severely.

I was so pleased with him that I told him what Betty Friske had said. "He might have given her a key!" Sean exclaimed.

"He might, but what worries me is why she wants to see him. She threatened him, Sean. What could she be going to the police about? I know perfectly well Victor didn't steal anything or something like that."

"How old is she?" he asked.

"The shady side of thirty-five, I'd say, but well preserved. Why?"

"Leave her to me. I have a way with older women."

"Older women go for that macho line, do they?" It was petty of me. "The balding head probably helps."

"Bald!" The howl caused heads to turn three tables away.

"I didn't say bald. Balding—there's a difference. You still have quite a bit of hair. You probably won't be bald for four or five years."

"Jeez, you really know how to wreck a guy's appetite," he complained and ate on with no noticeable decrease in either speed or pleasure.

Everything was just as we'd left it when we got back to the apartment including Victor's Corvette parked in the garage. I didn't see Betty's door open when we went into the apartment, and after about two minutes Sean said he was going down to talk to her. "I'd better put my hat on," he said, patting his hairline and glaring at me.

"And leave it on," I urged.

I kept my door ajar and heard him charm his way in like a snake oil salesman. He thickened up his accent a few degrees.

"Howdy, Ma'am," he said. "The name's Bradley, Sean Bradley. A friend of Victor Mazzini—the gentleman that lives next door. I can't seem to get a line on him. The rascal's run to ground and forgot to pay me a little old debt. It's only a couple of hundred, but I'm visiting in your fine city and find myself a bit short."

The next thing I heard was her door open and Sean's boots shuffle in. I waited ten minutes (twelve and a half, actually), and when he came back, his lower face was bruised.

"Now there is one lonesome lady!" he exclaimed and pulled out his handkerchief to wipe his brow. As the handkerchief was red with white polka dots, I couldn't see the lipstick on it, but I knew it would be there.

I swallowed down my revulsion and said, "Did you find out anything?"

"Oh yeah. Victor's hawking some jewelry for her. She gave

him a diamond ring and a bracelet, and she hasn't seen hide or hair of him since. Just three days ago, she handed them over. What do you make of it?"

"Harry Walton," I said, and explained. "He's a friend of Victor's who handles second hand jewelry. I'm sure my uncle wasn't planning to steal them."

"Why don't you give Harry a call and be sure?"

"I will."

I called Harry, and heard with a rush of relief that Victor had taken the ring and bracelet to him. He didn't have a buyer yet, but a woman was interested in the ring. Harry asked about Victor's disappearance; I said we hadn't found out much yet and hung up.

"It's funny Victor was selling Betty's jewelry. I thought he wasn't seeing her these days," I said.

"He goes over to her place when you're out. You're too young to scandalize with the affair. What I was wondering is whether she has a key. She said he goes there. I didn't like to ask her right out."

"I thought from your dislocated jaw you might be intimate enough to enquire."

"Not yet, but I'm working on it," he smiled softly. "Betty thinks bald men are sexy."

"Betty thinks all men are sexy. Betty is probably a nymphomaniac."

He smiled blissfully. "And I was afraid a Canadian holiday might be dull. Just goes to show you."

CHAPTER 6

"Do you think you could handle a drink, with those sore lips?"
I asked.

Sean oozed a leery smile at me. "A cold beer would hit the
spot," he agreed. "They could do with some cooling down."

It did hit the spot, and I was glad I had a little alcohol in me
when the phone rang. I only jumped one foot, instead of going
through the ceiling.

"This is Mr. Bartlett from the Bank of Montreal speaking,"
the disembodied voice announced—a flat, banker's voice.
"I've been reading of Mr. Mazzini's disappearance in the
papers. Have you had any word from him?"

Already a nervous upheaval was building under my ribs.
Banks weren't chummy enough to be making a purely social
call. I explained who I was, and told him no, we hadn't had
any word.

"I'm a little worried about his loan," he said, in a voice that
was more than just a little worried.

"Loan?" The nervous upheaval escalated to a quake.

"The loan he arranged last week. It's insured against his
death, of course, but in the case of a disappearance, I—well
quite frankly, Miss Newton, I don't know what to do. I'm the
Loan Manager. I personally approved the loan and now to have
him disappear . . ." His tone implied it was pretty shabby
behaviour on Victor's part.

I gulped and said, "I'm sure he'll turn up soon. How much
is the loan for?"

"I can't divulge that information over the phone."

Bankers understand money as surely as Betty Friske understands sex, so I tried a little guile on him. "I see. I thought perhaps you wanted me to meet the payments in his absence."

There was interest in his reply, but doubt was paramount. How did he know by my voice I was penniless? "It was a rather large loan."

"How large?"

"As I said, I can't divulge that over the phone."

Sean, listening at my shoulder, covered the receiver with his hand and said, "We can go down in person." I relayed this to Mr. Bartlett, and a meeting was arranged for as soon as we could get there. His eagerness gave rise to shattering worries about the size of Victor's loan.

Since my uncle used the closest bank, it was hardly more than an elevator ride away.

"He won't tell me anything if you're along," I pointed out to Sean. "He wouldn't even tell me, and I'm Victor's niece."

"I'm your fiancé," he decided. "Maybe you better let me do the talking."

Help was one thing, and appreciated, but taking over was less welcome. This was a family matter, and he sounded like he didn't think I could handle it. "No, maybe I better not!" He took my decision quietly, so I let him tag along.

Mr. Bartlett looked more prepossessing than his voice had led me to imagine. He was tall, a slender man with graying hair and tinted glasses. He wore a dark suit, even in summer, and had a private office of sorts, the privacy diluted by a glass wall from the waist up.

I introduced Sean as my fiancé, and rushed on to do the talking myself. I figured an appeal to Bartlett's greed was my best lever, and outlined that my uncle would be greatly embarrassed to have his financial reputation stained by not meeting his loan payments, so if he'd just tell me how much the payment would be, and when it was due, I'd sell some securities (this I managed without a blush) and make the payment for him. Was it due now?

"Oh no! Not till the middle of July. He only arranged the loan a week ago. It's these distressing stories in the newspapers that have caused the alarm. As I said, it was rather a large loan," he added, brows raised. A man probably in charge of millions, and he was as scared as a jackrabbit.

"Over a million?" Sean asked nonchalantly. He had turned on the Texas accent for the occasion. "I don't know as I see my way clear to handling anything over a million, darlin'," he added in an apologetic aside to me.

"Dear me, no! Not a million!" Mr. Bartlett exclaimed, and laughed aloud with relief. "More in the amount of a hundred thousand. *Over* one hundred thousand," he added importantly.

Sean smiled and tossed up his hands. "No problem. It might help us locate Mr. Mazzini if you'd let us have a look at his account. I reckon he deposited the money in his account here. If he drew a check on it, it'll give us an idea what he did with the money and hopefully a lead on where we can find him."

"But he didn't take a check. He asked for cash," Mr. Bartlett said, and I believe he regretted the disclosure as soon as he'd made it.

"Cash! Isn't that very unusual?" I asked.

"Highly irregular, but Mr. Mazzini has always been a rather—unusual customer. Not to say he doesn't repay when he overdraws, but the artistic temperament . . ." He hunched his narrow shoulders forgivingly. "I thought it had to do with opening a Swiss account, or something of that sort," he added, looking to the Texas tycoon for agreement.

Sean nodded obligingly, as if he had a few million stashed in Switzerland himself. "How much over a hundred thousand?" he asked. To reproduce his accent would be impossible. It was Texan and broadly drawn.

"He asked for two hundred thousand. I couldn't see my way clear to letting him have that much. Of course he has good collateral. He borrowed between one and two hundred thousand—halfway between," he said, giving us the total in this oblique way, and with some anxiety that he was straying from the path of banking rectitude.

I blanched. "Now don't you worry your pretty little head about a thing, darlin'," Sean told me.

We all three sat looking at each other for a minute, then Sean gave a jerk of the head, and I began the ritual of leaving, thanking Mr. Bartlett, and assuring him the loan was in no jeopardy. As Mr. Bartlett wasn't aware of the insignificant nature of my bank balance and the spurious nature of Sean's accent and fortune, he looked relieved.

"A real pleasure to meet you, sir," Sean said and clamped Bartlett's hand.

He took my arm, and we hustled out to the street. "At least we know what's being looked for now," I said.

"He got the loan a week ago. Do you think he was still carrying around the cash?"

Upon consideration, it sounded unlikely. Why borrow such a huge sum, only to pay the interest on it? Obviously he had some immediate need for the money. As the European tour wasn't till the autumn, it seemed logical he'd borrow in the autumn, if he meant to stash the money in a Swiss account. But surely people didn't borrow money to put in a Swiss account. They were for people with money to spare, money to hide from the taxman.

"On the off chance that Victor's bank book might give us a clue to this, shall we go back up to his studio?" I suggested.

"My thoughts exactly."

Inside the main doorway, I suddenly glanced at the locked mail boxes. The mailman didn't arrive till after I left for work, so I usually got my letters from the mahogany table by the front door, but Victor had given me a key, and I used it to pick up the mail before going upstairs. There was a letter from Mom to me, some bills and a letter in a Royal York Hotel envelope for my uncle. It had a paper inside, with something hard wrapped in it. The most intriguing thing about it, however, was that the handwriting on the envelope was Victor's. There was no mistaking his bold, flashy scrawl. The postmark was Toronto, and the date of mailing was yesterday. It temporarily put the bank statement out of my mind.

"There's something funny here," I muttered. Before the elevator reached the seventeenth floor, we had torn the envelope open. Wrapped inside a piece of Royal York stationery was a plain metal key with the number 87 on it.

"It's from some kind of a locker," Sean said.

"The Royal York connects underground to Union Station. There are baggage lockers there," I told him. My heart quickened. "I arrived there by train from Montreal and used them. This looks like the right kind of key."

We went through the formality of checking out the apartment for signs of trespassing or Victor's return—both negative—before we went tearing down to Union Station. "The subway would be faster," Sean mentioned. "It goes right to the station."

It always surprised me how quickly other people got their bearings in a strange city. We went to the bus stop to grab a bus to the subway. "How long have you been visiting here?" I asked him.

"A week now," he said, which surprised me. In some unreasonable way I pictured him arriving just before we met at the Casa Loma.

As we jostled along on the bus to the subway I said, "I guess you've seen all the sights by now then, huh?"

"I've been looking around," he said vaguely. "I went up to the top of that tower, the CN Tower they call it. I saw the Parliament Buildings at Queen's Park, been out to Ontario Place and down to the Harbour Front. Oh, and the Eaton Centre, of course. We've got a mall a lot like it in North Platte, only a bit smaller."

Our time together had been nearly totally occupied with looking for Victor, but during the lulls, I'd been forming some plan of showing Sean the town after we found my uncle to reward him for his help. I felt gypped. I should have realized the Casa Loma wouldn't be the first item on a visitor's agenda.

"There's a lot more to see," I said.

"I'd like to catch a Blue Jays game."

Next to fishing, baseball is the dullest thing I could think of.

Sean had already learned his way around the subway. He even had a pocketful of metal tokens. He negotiated the maze at the terminal without any difficulty at all, down escalators and up stairs, till we reached the bank of luggage lockers.

We both paid lip service to the idea that the hundred and fifty thousand dollars had been spent or invested, but I, for one, also had a firm idea it was resting in cubicle 87 and could hardly speak for the walloping of my heart.

Our key opened locker 87, and there sitting in the square cubicle was Victor's well-battered black violin case. Nothing else, just the case. Sean lifted it out with a wary look over his shoulder, looking for God only knows what, except that it seemed a climactic enough moment for some crook to jump out at us.

"His violin," I said, bewildered.

"We'd better open this in some private place," Sean suggested. His eyes were sparkling like fire crackers.

"Why, it's only his violin, isn't it?" He looked doubtful. "I'll take it to the ladies' washroom," I decided, and reached for it.

He didn't let go. "That's a little too private. I want you to be where I can keep an eye on you. For your safety, I mean," he added hastily. He caught the swift rise of suspicion in my eyes. Why should he want to "keep an eye on me"? "There's something in it all right, but it doesn't feel like a violin." He gave it a little shake, by the handle. I could hear a louder rattle than the violin made.

"Does it feel like a hundred and fifty thousand bucks?"

He gave a triumphant smile. "Sure does—wrapped in two bundles."

My impatience soared. I wanted to rip it open right then and there. "Couldn't we go up to your room?"

"My room?" he asked, frowning.

"Aren't you putting up at the Royal York?"

"Where'd you get that idea?"

"I don't know. You just seemed the Royal York type."

"What type is that?"

Safe, solid, middleclass was what I thought, but I said, "North Platte type."

Sean was hardly listening. He said, "There must be a quiet bar in a big hotel. One that's nice and dark, and not too well populated in the early afternoon."

"The Library Bar!"

"I see you know all the watering holes."

"A person has to drink."

We hurried up the stairs, through a maze of corridors to the red plush lobby of the Royal York, around corners into the Library Bar, which was as dark, private and as unpopulated as even a spy could hope for. There were only two tables occupied, both by unsuspicious touristy couples.

The waiter was at our table before we had the violin case

arranged on the padded bench between us. Sean ordered two beers without asking me what I wanted.

"Light," I added. Even light beer had more calories than I needed. I wanted to save my calories for chocolate cake.

As soon as the waiter left, Sean unfastened the clasps and slowly lifted the lid of the case. It was crushed gold velvet inside, to cushion the Guarneri. My rundown Adidas looked extremely out of place in such an elegant setting. That's what was in the case. Wads of paper were squashed into balls to fill up the two ends to prevent the shoes from rattling around in there.

"Well I'll be a son of a stockbroker," Sean breathed, staring at the shoes. "A pair of dirty old shoes. Not even Victor's size. He must have plucked them from somebody's garbage."

"No, he plucked them from my locker at the Casa Loma. I used to put them on at noon sometimes and walk around the grounds a bit for exercize. He must have taken them yesterday when he dropped in to see me. He used the employees' washroom, close to the lockers."

"What's all this garbage?" Sean asked, and began pulling out the wadded papers. There were a few copies of the Casa Loma tour booklet, also taken from the locker probably, but most of the space was filled with paper towels from the wash room. That's when he filled the case all right, while he was in the john.

When the waiter approached, Sean discreetly closed the lid. We sipped the beer in silence, too stunned to talk. It takes a few minutes to accept such a bizarre thing as either a violin or a hundred and fifty thousand dollars changing into a pair of old Adidas.

Sean ran his hand through his hair. "This has got to be the worst exchange since Jack sold his mother's cow for a handful of beans."

"Maybe we should plant them and grow an Adidas tree," I said lamely. You say some pretty dumb things when you're baffled, but I don't think he heard me.

His eyes were narrowed, which gave his face a crafty, shifty look. "It looks as if Victor lost his nerve," he said.

"I don't get it. You think he was afraid to give the concert? That he ducked out for fear the critics would think he wasn't playing well? You're wrong. He'd been practicing his fingers off. I'm not an expert, but he sounded pretty good to me."

"I was thinking about something else—the money. I thought that's what was in the case. Maybe somebody else was supposed to think so too. Maybe Victor was supposed to exchange the money for—something—some object he was going to buy. Maybe he planned to pull a fast one, give the guy a case full of old running shoes and lost his nerve."

"That's a lot of maybes," I snorted. "Maybe you're suggesting my uncle is a crook, too. Well he isn't!"

"Then how do you account for the contents of this case?" he demanded, eyes flashing, as he thumped the case with his flat palm.

"I don't account for them. It's not my job. It's a job for the police, and the police station is my next stop." Though I spoke firmly, I felt a strange reluctance. I'd been swift to defend Victor, but Sean's idea caused a seed of suspicion to sprout in me. I didn't believe Sean's version of the story, but some slightly larcenous trick wasn't entirely beyond Victor.

"He said he was on his way to Roy Thomson Hall yesterday when he stopped in to see you?" he asked. His eyes were bright, alert not only with suspicion but with intelligence. He reminded me of a squirrel, fidgety, eager to be darting off somewhere.

"Yes, but the manager said he didn't go. He obviously came here instead—to the lockers at Union Station." I gnawed at this puzzle a while till I came up with a cockeyed notion. "Do you think he might have been taking the money somewhere and thought somebody was following him? So he took it out at the Casa Loma and hid it and stuffed the case with papers and running shoes?"

I was pleased with this piece of invention. Its greatest charm was that it gave us a new place to look for the money. Or violin—depending on what Victor originally had in the case. At least it was something to explore.

"But why check the case at Union Station?" he countered.

"Why not? Whoever was following him would think he'd checked the money and stop following him. It would be pretty hard to crack one of those lockers open without getting caught. But how did anyone know he borrowed all that money and had it in cash? Sean, maybe it's the *key* someone's been searching for ever since!" I exclaimed. I smiled widely at this stroke of genius.

Sean gave me a jaundiced look. "We decided it was something bigger that was being searched for."

"*You* decided. A key could be hidden in a cupboard or under a sofa cushion."

"He didn't pull off the sofa cushions. He pulled the sofas out from the wall and looked behind them. Both at the apartment and at the cottage. And under the beds—nobody would hide a key under a bed," he said firmly. "Under a mattress, maybe . . ."

I smiled a smug, superior smile. "You're slipping, Sean. Better run home and read another Sherlock Holmes book. I thought you'd have picked up on something else before now."

"What's that?" A smile of anticipation lifted his moustache.

"If Victor hid the money at Casa Loma, it must still be there," I pointed out. "And I even know more or less where it must be," I added triumphantly. But I still had that one niggling doubt that all we'd find was his old violin.

"In your locker?"

"No, I don't have a lock for it, but it must be somewhere in that general area. There are dozens of possibilities."

He pulled a bill from his pocket, picked up the violin case and we ran off with our beer half drunk, leaving too large a tip.

CHAPTER 7

During the cab drive to the Casa Loma, I was hardly aware of the towers of glass and concrete and steel rising around us. The city looked like a gigantic hall of mirrors, with sun glinting everywhere, reflecting from the buildings.

"They're going to wonder why I'm not at work when I'm unworried enough about Victor to be out running around the city," I told him.

"Couldn't you have left something important in your locker? That's the area we want to snoop around."

"You're a real good liar, Sean," I said.

He ignored the ambivalence in this praise. "I have many accomplishments," he said modestly.

"You'd think a hardware salesman would be more reliable. Salt of the earth, I always took them for. I often wished they could speak English. Whenever I've been in a hardware store, the men talk about two-b'fours and ratchets and jigsaws. How come you never talk about two-b'fours?"

"I'm on holiday. A man likes to forget ratchets and jigsaws once a year. Will we have to pay to get in?"

"Of course not." But the question made me aware that Sean was spending a lot of money on my problem. And a clerk in a hardware store couldn't make much. "Listen, Sean, I don't want you to get all uptight and macho, but I want to repay you for all the expense you've been put to on my account. There've been taxis and meals and drinks and the trip to Victor's cottage . . ." As the total began to tally up, I saw the tab was becoming quite high.

His easy smile showed me he wasn't quite broke yet. "I'll bill you, okay?"

He was too quaint to be comfortable talking money, but the man hasn't been born who'll turn down a home-cooked meal. I don't know how to cook and have no desire to learn, but I knew a caterer who would bring food to the apartment. Victor used them when his company menu was beyond Rhoda Gardiner.

"All right, but tonight dinner's at my place."

He looked uncomfortable; more than uncomfortable, he looked extremely reluctant. My pride felt the unpleasant sting of rejection. "Thanks for the offer, but I'm not really into bean sprouts and tofu," he said apologetically.

"What? Oh, you mean because I'm a vegetarian. Actually since I've been living with Victor, I've had to recant a little. I can't expect Rhoda to make two meals, so I just close my eyes and eat meat."

Relief rose like the sun on his face. "Oh, you mean you were lying. Thank God! It's a date then. Are you a good cook?"

"I bake a few beans," I said airily.

We stopped for a minute outside the castle to admire it like all the tourists. It stands high atop a hill in palatial grounds, an unlikely gray stone structure with a tiled roof. When he had it built, Sir Henry Pellatt scoured Europe and had added every feature he could think of. There are battlements and minarets, a port cochère, gothic arches—a regular hodgepodge of grandeur, more suited to the banks of the Rhine than the heart of Toronto.

The interior is also bizarre, anachronistic and grand. The Great Hall has dark wainscotting for eight or nine feet up the wall, a fireplace, pictures and armour and staghorns. There's a billiard room, breakfast room, dining room, and one called The Oak Room (to name a few), and below ground level the magnificence continues with a temperature-controlled wine cellar, an eight-hundred-foot-long tunnel to the stables that are another mansion in themselves. Why horses need stalls of Spanish mahogany and walls of glazed tile is not included in our spiel, but it certainly impresses the patrons.

Tours were in progress when we arrived, and a new one was forming. I told the ticket taker who knew me that I just had to pick up something from my locker and took Sean's hand, pulling him in with me. I didn't have to answer a single question about Victor or anything else. None of the higher ups were around, so I led Sean to the locker area, and we began looking for the money, or failing that, Victor's violin. We agreed it must be in a bag or box.

Sean, being taller, stood on his toes and felt along the tops of the lockers while I scavenged through them and the cupboards built in along the sides of the room. The guides had a little kitchenette here, with crockery and supplies. It took me five minutes to feel every bag and open every canister.

"You might have a look in the men's john after you're through there," I told Sean. "If he hid it in the waste towel basket hoping to retrieve it later, we're out of luck. It'd be emptied and thrown out by now."

He darted along to the men's room, while I finished my fruitless search of the employees' room. When I joined Sean in the hall, he was still empty-handed too.

"The towel basket hadn't been emptied—it was damned near overflowing. I emptied it on the floor and went through it towel by towel. I had to scrub myself raw after in case of germs," he complained. "I even looked inside all the water tanks on top of the toilets—*The Godfather*, remember? It wasn't there in an oilskin bag, either."

"I figured you'd have told me if you found it."

"It wasn't in the new paper towel dispenser. There aren't that many places to look in a can. What's down this way?" He glanced along the long, dimly lit hall that runs to the rear of the castle.

"I don't know. I've never been down there." It proved to be a back door into the place which required a quick search of the bushes outside, also without luck.

"Any more bright ideas?" he asked, becoming impatient.

"He took a scoot up to the Music Room, but he couldn't have left it there in such a public place. There would have been hundreds of people through it. The last tour was on its way through yesterday when he was here. Do you want to look anyway?"

"It'll save coming back later."

One of the guides was just ushering her group through the Music Room. We hung behind after she left, but the public nature of the room left little hope of a find here. The Steinway grand was roped off to keep tourists from trying to play it. There were other instruments set artfully around the room as well: a harp, a cello, a violin propped on its case on the piano. We both had the brilliant idea at the same time that the violin was Victor's, but when we hopped the rope and took a look, we saw it was just the same old instrument that had been there forever. It was nothing like Victor's. I'd seen the room a few dozen times, and nothing was disarranged. The heavy brocade drapes had solidified to a texture not unlike concrete. The long case clock by the door still said seven-fifteen, as it did throughout the day.

We exchanged a disappointed look and left. The afternoon was well advanced when we left the castle. "It's a dead end," I said. Despair was pushing at the back of my mind, or maybe desperation is what I mean. "I'm going back to the apartment and just wait in case Victor phones or comes home. Sean, you don't really think anything horrible has happened to him, do you?"

Sean was looking down the road for a cab. He took my hand and we began walking along, both scanning the road. I felt tears smarting my eyes and was stricken with a terrible fear that my uncle really was dead. Before much longer, I'd be arranging a funeral for him. He'd want a neon funeral, if there is such a thing. Oh, I wasn't fool enough not to know his death was possible before, but it had seemed only remotely possible. I always thought his disappearance was a gag, a gimmick cooked up by my uncle, but as I looked back over the accumulating evidence, that looked less likely all the time.

Close to twenty-four hours had passed since his disappearance, and there was still no word from him. The apartment had been searched, the cottage had been searched, and there was this bizarre business of a loan for a hundred and fifty thousand dollars in cash. Why did Victor need so much money? It was no gimmick. He could have hired a revolution for less. And there was the violin case with my Adidas in it that jostled against Sean's knee as we walked along. What had Victor done with his Guarneri? That was as confusing as all the rest.

"At least we know he was safe at Union Station yesterday. Pretty hard for anybody to kidnap him at Union Station, or the hotel where he mailed himself the key. They're both busy spots," Sean said to reassure me, but I wasn't reassured. A crowd could conceal quite effectively.

Another of my unfounded images popped into my head. Victor with a gun nuzzled against his spine, a jacket over the weapon to conceal it from onlookers. Had he fallen afoul of the mob? Were the loan sharks after him? The thought was so upsetting that I shook it away. Sean suddenly stopped walking and turned toward me. He wore a Eureka! look. "I wonder if he would have caught a train since he was at the station!" he exclaimed.

"If he did, we'll never be able to trace him. The Go trains for commuters leave at that time. The crowd's like Macy's on sale day."

"But is there a train to Caledon, to his cottage?"

"Not directly, and besides, he wasn't at the cottage. He drove the car home to the apartment after he was at the station. I wonder what Thomson Hall is doing about tonight's concert. I haven't had the radio or TV on all day. I'm going home to do that now." The back of my neck ached from the strain of the day's tension. I felt muggy all over. I wanted to sink into a warm tub and feel the lap of clean water over my naked body.

"Do you want some company?" he offered. I was a little surprised till I remembered I'd only thought about the bath—I hadn't said it aloud.

We came to the corner and stopped. I took a good long look at Sean. "Some holiday you're having," I said, and squeezed his fingers. "I'm sure glad you're here. I don't know what I'd have done alone." I meant every word of it. Looking at his reassuring square jaw, his friendly brown eyes, lit now with sympathy, I wanted to kiss him in gratitude.

"I'm glad, too," he said. "It's not every day a nuts and bolts guy like me gets a chance to help a damsel in distress. It'll be okay, Cassie. I don't see any reason why anybody would kill him. You get into murder—especially of a celebrity—you're asking for big trouble. He's just locked up somewhere, and what we've got to do is get busy and find him."

"That's all, huh?" My bottom lip wobbled unsteadily. The tears were about two seconds away, ready to spurt if he said one more sympathetic word. I didn't feel right about Sean, using up his holiday on him. He'd probably saved all year for this vacation, maybe two or three years. But I sure didn't want to be alone for this ordeal, either.

"What time will I call for you?" he asked when we spotted an empty taxi cruising forward.

The question surprised and cheered me until I remembered I had promised him dinner. "How does seven suit you?"

"It suits me just fine." The cab pulled in at the curb, and we climbed in.

In the taxi he put his arm around me and I leaned my head on his chest, not speaking. His fingers felt good, massaging the tension from my neck. I wanted to close my eyes and go to sleep and stay asleep till Victor came back, but it was only a short drive to the apartment. Sean gave me his phone number as we pulled up in front of the building.

"Where are you staying?" I asked.

"I'm at a little inn downtown, but I noticed something called the Park Plaza Hotel quite close to your place. I think I might move."

I was touched by his thoughtfulness, but felt I should warn him. "That's pretty expensive, Sean," I said as he climbed out of the taxi and held the door for me.

He smiled reassuringly. "That's all right. I soak them real good on the nuts and bolts."

"Oh, do you *own* the store?" I shouldn't have let myself sound so shocked and so delighted.

He gave a modest little blush that was very endearing. "It's not very big, but I own it." He really was such a sweet man. I was going to order dinner that would blow his sox off, and that would take some dinner, when there was a pair of very tall western boots that had to blow before the sox.

"Try not to worry," he said, just before he got back in the cab. I wanted to offer to pay the bill, or at least split it, but I knew his Nebraska blood would be offended, so I kissed him on the cheek instead, and he handed me the violin case.

The last glimpse I had of him through the window, he was smiling like a teenager with his first set of wheels. I felt insensibly cheered to know he'd be coming back in a few hours. Being human, I also wondered just how small his "little" store was and realized very well the impossibility of being either a diplomat or Sybarite in North Platte, Nebraska. I wouldn't even have anyone to speak French to. *C'était trop mal, ça.*

CHAPTER 8

I had the very best intention of providing Sean a Grade A gourmet dinner. The restaurant had duck à l'orange and everything that they'd deliver. That we eventually ended up eating leftovers at nine o'clock was not my fault. The phone was ringing when I stepped into the apartment, and between it and the doorbell, I didn't have time to draw a breath, much less plan our gourmet meal. During my absence, Victor's disappearance had escalated to a city-wide scandal.

The first call was from Rhoda asking if Mr. Mazzini was back yet, and when I said no, she asked if she should come in tomorrow. I was uncertain how much privacy my quest for Uncle Victor might require. Casting an eye around the apartment, I decided it could go another day without dusting and gave her the day off. I hadn't got more than two steps away from the phone when it rang again. That time it was Eleanor.

"Is there any word, Cassie?" she asked in her throaty voice that sounds as though her vocal chords had been marinated in brandy and smoke.

"No, nothing."

"I've been calling and calling all day long. Where on earth have you been?" she asked accusingly.

"Out looking for my uncle."

"Where?" she asked, mystified.

"All over. I drove up to the cottage," I said, as a for instance.

69

"That shouldn't have taken all day. What are you going to tell the press?" was her next question.

I was surprised at the trivial nature of her concern. "I'm not planning to tell them anything."

She asked me a few more fairly pointless questions, and as soon as I got rid of her, the phone rang again. It was a reporter from the least respectable of the newspapers wanting the inside story on Victor's disappearance. How did he get an unlisted number? Victor had probably sent it around to all the newspapers and radio and TV stations. "No comment," I said briskly and hung up.

Those newspapermen have ways and means of inveigling themselves into places they're not wanted. He must have been calling from somewhere nearby and sneaked into the building on the coattails of a legitimate resident. I only had time to take my Adidas out of the violin case and stick the case in Victor's studio when the reporter appeared at the door in person, scaring the life out of me.

I was trembling when I looked out the peephole at a man I'd never seen in my life before. The fact that he had a pen and pad in his hand alerted me to his probable identity, and I didn't let him in. He stayed there for ages, ringing and trying to talk through the door, asking questions. His persistence brought Betty Friske out, and he walked down the hall to talk to her.

While he was still there, the phone rang again. It was the manager of Roy Thomson Hall, also giving me hell for not being home all day to answer the phone. Naturally he was curious to know whether Victor planned to perform for the evening concert. Did I realize the media and orchestra had to be notified if the performance was to be cancelled? What could I say? I said I still hadn't heard from Mr. Mazzini and suggested that any sane manager would have taken the necessary steps to cancel hours ago.

The oddest thing of all was that the police didn't come or even phone, but my reaction at the time was relief. My boss from Casa Loma phoned—I'd given him the phone number myself—and agreed that I shouldn't return to work tomorrow. He was very understanding. I managed to read Mom's letter between calls—no important news there. Twice I remembered Victor's bank statement and even got it from his studio, but before I had a chance to examine it, the phone was ringing again, so I stuffed the statement into my purse and picked up the receiver. Two friends from work called, and Ronald Strathroy arrived in person at five-thirty, hot from Bay Street.

The well-oiled machine was less smooth this evening. His face looked drawn with little smudges beneath his eyes. Ronald wasn't a very demonstrative person, but as soon as he was inside the door, he took my hands and kissed me lightly on the lips.

"Poor Cassie," he said, with a gentle smile, "this must be hell for you. I've tried a dozen times to get hold of you on the phone today. Where have you been?"

I squeezed his fingers while he gazed into my eyes. I was touched to see the very real concern there. I had misjudged Ronald. His British air of frost hid his feelings, but he had them.

"I drove up to Caledon, looking for Victor." This didn't seem the optimum time to mention Sean Bradley.

"No luck, I take it?"

"Someone had been there, but I don't think it was my uncle." I told him about the hasty search.

"It's such a strange thing," he puzzled, walking me to the sofa with an arm around my waist. We sat down, and he ran a hand through his smooth wheat-silk hair, dishevelling it attractively.

"It's weird. Can I get you something to drink, Ron?"

"A Scotch would hit the spot."'

I made him a Scotch and soda and took a straight soda water for myself to control the calories. It was companionable, chatting with him on the sofa, his fingers just brushing my shoulder. The only discomfort was that time was ticking past, and I had to decide on and order dinner for Sean and pull myself into presentable shape. But there was time for a sociable drink at least.

"What did the police have to say this morning?" he asked.

I outlined their questions and my answers in less than two minutes. It was perfectly natural that he should next ask what else had occurred during the day, and though I felt some urge to tell him everything, I hedged. Whatever Victor was up to, I wanted to keep it in the family. My uncle had roamed the world

long enough. Toronto was what he now called home, and he
liked being a part of the established society. Eleanor Strathroy
was his lifeline to it, and I didn't want to sever this vital
connection. So I spoke vaguely of the phone calls I had
received within the past half hour, letting him think they had
come over the space of the whole day.

"But you were out this afternoon when I called," he said.

"I had to go to the bank."

"It's rough, your being here alone during all this. Why don't
you go and spend a few days with Mom?" he suggested.
"She'd be delighted to have you."

Every city has an exclusive area like Forest Hill where the
old rich built stone mansions in the days when it was still
possible, and their lucky descendants now have the luxury of
living in them, close to the heart of a large city. I'd been to the
Strathroys' for a few dinners and parties and knew how
formally they lived. When I thought of being a jet setter
myself, I didn't mean to run with that pack. I was interested in
the livelier set. Actually nouveau riche would suit me better.
But it was kind of him to offer, and I refused kindly.

"I should stay here where I can handle the messages that
come pouring in. I have to be available to Roy Thomson Hall
and the police, and of course Victor, too, if he tries to get in
touch with me. Or in case it's a kidnapper, you know . . ." I
let it hang heavy in the air.

"Don't think that, Cassie," he said and took my hand again.
"No one would kidnap Victor. He's a man of great genius, but
he isn't wealthy. Criminals only kidnap for money."

"That's true." I felt badly, keeping so much secret from
Ronald. He was my oldest friend in the city. Here I was sharing
my troubles with a total stranger when a good friend was at
hand.

When he spoke again, it was about Sean, though Ronald
didn't know his name. "Mom mentioned you were with some
man at the concert last night." He didn't sound jealous exactly,
though there was a little of that mixed with the curiosity.

I downplayed Sean. "He's just a tourist—an American I met
at work yesterday. He was sorry he had to miss Victor's
concert, and since I had your ticket right in my purse, I gave

it to him. I didn't actually go with him—the seat was just next to mine."

"Did you know him before, or was he just a chance acquaintance?"

"I'd never seen him in my life till yesterday. He's a hardware salesman from Nebraska."

"Oh, I see." This killed the last shred of Ronald's interest. "What do you want to do tonight? Would you like me to stay here with you since you don't feel you can leave? I don't want you to be alone." Concern and sympathy were in his eyes. I hoped the impatience wasn't too visible in mine.

"You look tired out, Ron. You must be, too, after your trip yesterday. Why don't you go home and get a good sleep? I'll be fine."

"No, no, I insist. I don't want to leave you alone, all worried and nervous."

"I'm not nervous. I have dozens of things to do. I have to write to Mom."

"Let me take you out for dinner at least. You can leave for an hour," he urged.

I invented a late lunch and finally persuaded him I wasn't a basket case yet. He finished his Scotch and put down his glass. "If you change your mind, give me a ring," he said. "I'll go home now. Mom's in a state, too. Remember now, call us if you hear anything. Or even if you just get lonesome. We'll keep in touch."

I went to the door with him, trying not to hurry my steps. "Sweet Cassie," he said softly, and stopped at the door to pull me into his arms for a kiss. This one wasn't a peck; it lasted a few minutes and made me forget all about Sean and dinner.

I was troubled after he left. This was a considerate, thoughtful side of Ronald I hadn't seen before. During our half dozen or so dates, I never felt he really liked me. I was always a little on edge with Ronald, a little too aware of the difference in our backgrounds, but he was proving a good friend. We'd be closer after this Victor affair was over.

But my immediate concern was to phone the restaurant and order dinner. I looked up the number and sat thinking what food would suit a hardware salesman from Nebraska without adding a zillion calories to a dieter. I didn't know one single person from Nebraska unless you could count Johnny Carson or Dick Cavett. Maybe duck à l'orange was too pretentious, but a steak wouldn't travel well. Something with a sauce that could be slipped into the oven for a few minutes before serving . . .

I was at the phone about to order coq au vin for two to go when the doorbell sounded once more. I thought it might be one of the neighbors since Victor was popular in the building. When I peeked out the peephole, I saw Fred Marven, the plainclothes policeman, standing there. My insides were shaking like a leaf in the wind when I admitted him.

"Have you found him?" I asked, staring.

"No, Ma'am, I'm afraid we haven't," he said, and stepped in, looking all around.

I led him to the sofa where he immediately spotted the two glasses. "A friend just dropped in," I said, before he spoke.

"I saw Mr. Strathroy in the parking garage," he said, which gave me hope for his alertness and ability to put two and two together. "I believe he was here this morning as well?"

"Yes, he dropped in on his way to work." I was proud to announce my connection with such local worthies. "The Strathroys are very good friends of the family."

"A fine family, the Strathroys. Have you and your uncle known them long?"

"Mr. Mazzini has known them longer than I have. I believe he met them a few years ago in Italy. Mrs. Strathroy's cousin lives there—married to an Italian." This all seemed highly irrelevant, but I wasn't eager to quit such a harmless topic. "He looked Mrs. Strathroy up when he moved to Toronto, and they became good friends."

We discussed the Strathroys for a while—Eleanor's party mainly—then he stirred in his seat. I was alarmed till I discovered what he wanted.

"I don't have a search warrant, but would you have any objection to my taking a look around the apartment?" he asked.

"Not at all. Go right ahead."

He began walking around, poking at everything, while I paced behind him. I took the idea he was looking for the money. I didn't know whether Mr. Bartlett, in a fit of timidity, had called the police, or the police had been checking into

Victor's financial affairs, but I don't know what else he could have been looking for. I remembered with a sigh of relief that I had put the bank statement into my purse.

He went into Victor's bedroom and sort of half closed the door behind him. This looked like a hint that he wanted to be alone, so I stayed outside. When he came out, he didn't mention the empty humidor. Next it was the studio. The only worrisome item there was the empty violin case. He didn't find it suspicious, or didn't mention it in any case. He stopped at my bedroom door and looked a question at me.

"That's all right. I gave the maid the day off, so you'll have to pardon the unmade bed." And my being a lazy slob.

The whole visit lasted only fifteen minutes. Marven was quick, but I don't know how efficient he was. At the doorway I screwed up my courage and asked, "Was there anything in particular you were looking for?"

He gave a bright, tight little smile. "Evidence," he said, "but I didn't find any. If you notice Mr. Mazzini's car missing from the garage, don't worry about it. We're removing it for the time being."

"Why?"

"Its ownership is in question now."

"Does he owe money on it?"

"No, he paid cash. You weren't aware he was selling his car?"

I blinked in disbelief. "He didn't mention it."

"He advertised it in the papers last week. A man put a thousand dollars down and was to bring Mr. Mazzini the remainder today and arrange the transfer of ownership papers. When he heard of your uncle's disappearance, he came down to the station and told us. The car is in the process of being sold, so it wouldn't be wise for you to drive it in case of an accident. It won't inconvenience you?"

"No, I never drive it, but . . ."

"You mustn't be concerned, Miss Newton. I expect your uncle planned to buy a different car. Good day."

Marven bowed himself out quite formally, and I stood, mute with shock. Victor couldn't be selling his car. He loved it. One of his greatest joys was crouching behind the wheel of that low-slung, showoff car with his silly little tweed cap pulled down over his eyes. His car was his second most precious possession after his Guarneri. And what had become of it?

I really couldn't settle down to arranging the dinner party after that. I didn't even get changed. When Sean came, I was still sitting in my dotted cotton dress, staring at my toes, which peeped out from my strapped sandals and noticing that my toenails could do with a new paint job.

Sean had done all the grooming I intended to do. He was freshly showered, shaved and dowsed in Old Spice. He had changed into a white sports shirt, open at the neck, with a light summer jacket over it. I could see the question in his eyes as he surveyed my frazzled state.

"What the hell's been going on here?" he demanded. His voice was sharp with worry, and his eyes darted over me as if he expected to see blood or bruises.

"What hasn't?" I asked, dazed. "Come on in and I'll tell you about it if I can remember it all. The phone hasn't stopped ringing since I came in except when I was answering the door. Everybody's been in touch. Oh, Sean, I haven't had a minute to order—to make dinner," I whined and suddenly burst into tears of frustration and worry.

Some girls sniffle beautifully, the less fortunate sniffle like me. My eyes turn red, my nose runs, and I make rough, hiccuping sounds. All these unattractive manifestations were in full view now, so when Sean pulled me into his arms, I went readily, averting my wet eyes from his nice jacket. I felt his strong fingers, one hand cuddling my head against his shoulder, the other around my back, patting gently, as if he were burping a baby. It only made the hiccuping sobs worse.

"And I haven't even called Mom!" I said suddenly. Why had I thought of her? It was the gentle cradling that did it. I felt safe as a child in its mother's arms and as dependent.

"You'll call her tonight as soon as you settle down. It's all right, it's all right now," he soothed. "You just have a good nervous breakdown—you've earned it—then we'll pull you back together."

As the sniffles subsided, he stuffed a white handkerchief into my fingers. Even that struck me as significant. He'd changed from his red polka dot one to impress me. I blotted my eyes and nose and ran to the bathroom for larger repairs. I splashed cold water on my face, brushed my hair and cleaned my teeth. Clean teeth make you feel so much better about yourself. My eyes were still blotched with pink when I went back to the living room. Sean was looking at the coffee table with the two empty glasses on it.

"Ronald and I had a drink," I said.

"Is he a teetotaler? I know you're not."

"What have you been doing, sniffing the glasses?"

"Cases are made up of details."

"Then you'll be keenly interested to know I had the soda water. Canada Dry. Make of it what you will. Sean, Victor sold his car," I announced, and watched as his face fell in shock.

"I noticed it was gone from the garage. I figured the cops had hauled it away."

"They did. They were here too." In bits and pieces I outlined the harrowing couple of hours I had put in since he left. He was stunned, unable to grasp all the various calls and callers that had plagued me.

"I thought you had an unlisted phone number!"

"Friends and business associates have it."

"I see why I've been gypped out of my dinner," he mumbled.

"Would you like a beer? I'll make something as soon as I recuperate."

"I'll get it. You've had enough to do."

He went to the kitchen and came back with two bottles, already opened. Before he even sat down, the phone rang again.

"Let it ring. I'm on strike," I said, and lifted the cold bottle to my lips. The welcome bitter sting of beer tasted like ambrosia on my throat, all one hundred and fifty calories of it.

"I'll get it. It might be important," he said and answered it.

"What's that? For sale, you say?" Sean's eyes grew an inch, and his forehead corrugated in surprise. With his hand covering the mouthpiece he said, "Victor's got his cottage for sale. This guy says it's advertised in the *Star*."

A giggle of uncontrolled hysteria erupted from my mouth. It could as easily have been sobs, but it was giggles that came out. Sean handled the call. I heard him say offputting things, that he'd get in touch with the man tomorrow and listened as if from a vast distance. Victor was selling his life away. He'd probably sold his violin, too. That's why we couldn't find it. Maybe he and Betty Friske were planning to run away to Tahiti together since she was selling her jewelry. I hoped Victor hadn't sold the condo, or I'd be sitting on the street corner.

When Sean hung up, he made a beeline for the newspapers and rifled through them till he found Victor's ad. Sure enough, the property described was the cottage, and sure enough, the number to call was our unlisted number. Another treat to look forward to—an inundation of callers interested in buying the cottage. I could take no more.

"I resign from being Victor Mazzini's niece," I declared. "I'm going to move into the YWCA and become an orphan. Oh, Lord, I didn't phone Mom! I don't want her to hear about Victor on the TV."

"You're in no condition to phone right now," Sean said as he ripped the ad out of the newspaper. "What you need is some food."

"There's some chick. salad in the fridge. It will stave off starvation. Unfortunately, I ate all the choc. cake."

"What?" His look displayed some fear that I'd become unhinged.

He went into the kitchen, and I heard the homey sounds of the fridge door opening, water turned on, pans and dishes rattling. I should be there doing it, or at least helping, but I had bottomed out. When the phone rang again, I roused myself to answer it—another man interested in buying the cottage. I took his name and number and said the owner would be in touch; he had to go out of town for a few days.

My beer got itself drunk up quickly, and just as quickly I went to the kitchen and opened another hundred and fifty calories. "I'm not sure that chicken is still edible. It was leftovers yesterday," I warned.

"It tastes okay," he said, rustling in the bread box for buns and adding them to the table. Some tomatoes were nearly ripe on the windowsill, and he washed them before putting them on a dish with lettuce. I got the mayo from the fridge door and set the places. I'd abstain from the mayo to atone for the second beer.

"I meant to have a really nice dinner, Sean. I owe you one,

but before we eat, I'm going to phone Mom. My conscience is nagging me so I won't be able to enjoy this if I don't."

Mom was happy to hear from me, and hadn't heard the story of Victor's disappearance yet. "He's off on a binge again," she said with grim Italian resignation.

I thought it best to let her nurse this idea as the alternative was even worse. "I'm sure he'll turn up in a day or so," I said calmly and withheld all the other puzzling occurrences.

"He must be unhappy. Is it a woman?" she asked knowingly.

"He's seeing a woman, a very nice lady, but there's no trouble between them."

"She must be a saint or a fool. Let me know when he turns up. I'll give him a piece of my mind. He doesn't know when he's well off—he'll run himself right out of the business. Nobody will hire a sodden violinist, and it will ruin his technique. All those years of lessons! We all suffered to pay for that."

I knew the story by heart, and interrupted her. "I'll let you know as soon as I learn anything. And don't worry."

"Am I allowed to worry about *you?* You should be safe in Toronto. Nothing bad will happen to you there. Lots of nice Italian boys in Toronto, a whole community of them. Do you go to Little Italy? Maria's cousin is going to look you up— Alfredo his name is. Alfredo Danzo. A medical student. Have you got good warm clothing?"

She never could be convinced we had a summer up here. "Yes, I'm fine." We talked a little about my life and job before I hung up, feeling lonesome, and oddly protective about Mom, who had protected me from life's vagaries for so long.

"Soup's on!" Sean called when he heard me hang up.

I was glad he was there, just a room away, waiting for me. It was strange I felt so at home with him, and so out of place at Ronald's house. I already felt as if I had known Sean for years, maybe all my life. I knew he'd be standing, waiting to pull out my chair for me. I had a pretty good idea he'd strained his ears to overhear my phone conversation, and that he wouldn't let on he'd heard a single word when I went to the kitchen. He'd have a politely disinterested look, maybe ask if I got through to Mom.

"Did you get through to your mom all right?" he asked, hand poised disinterestedly to pull out my chair.

"Yes, I talked to her."

He misread my smile as pleasure at having done my duty, and I was so satisfied with him and my omniscience that I let him.

CHAPTER 9

It was only a so-so dinner, but in our advanced state of starvation, it tasted great. Neither the phone nor the doorbell rang once. It was late enough by then that I hoped the interruptions were over until morning. We talked more about all the happenings of the day while the coffee dripped.

"Sean, do you know what we didn't do!" I exclaimed suddenly.

"I forgot the cream," he said and started to get up for it.

"No, we forgot to check Victor's bankbook. Remember, we started up here this afternoon to do it, then we found that key in the mail and went dashing off to the station. I started to look at it half a dozen times but never got around to it."

"I bet the police took it," Sean said with a tsk of annoyance.

"No, they didn't. It's in my purse. I'll get it."

I brought it to the kitchen table, but it held no great surprises. One hundred and fifty thousand hadn't been deposited, of course. We knew he'd taken that in cash. There was a good advance for the concert—it went in and out the same day. It would have to be repaid now. The thousand-dollar down-payment on the Corvette was in and out, too. I had both his passbook and his personal book of matching entries, but there was nothing else startling.

Sean worried his lip as his eyes darted along the page. "If he was trying to accumulate a pool of cash, you'd never know it from this. Five hundred bucks for clothes! And look at this Visa payment! Something that required all that cash must have come up very suddenly to make him sell his car and cottage."

"You don't usually buy expensive things for cash," I said doubtfully. "Cash suggests something illegal. You don't think he was being blackmailed?" I asked, hardly conceiving it possible.

Sean examined me over the rim of his coffee cup. "For what? He can't be an illegal immigrant—his life's too public."

"No, it couldn't be that—he's had his citizenship for years. His little weaknesses are wine and women."

"And song," Sean added, probably because the three words are always linked in our minds.

"Music isn't illegal. Not even playing the violin. I mean unless you steal somebody else's composition and claim it for your own. And none of the stuff Victor claims as his own is good enough to bother stealing. He'd root around in old books and find something first class if he meant to pull off plagiarism."

"Maybe he wanted to buy something illegal," Sean suggested quietly. We were both racking our brains for an answer and coming up with some pretty farfetched ideas.

"He's not one of those crazy connoisseurs who'd buy stolen *objets d'art* for his own sole covetous enjoyment. If my uncle couldn't display his purchase to the world, he wouldn't buy it."

Sean still wore that quiet air, but there was a sharp look in his eyes that puzzled me. "Are you sure that applies across the board?"

"You're talking about women? That he does in private. Do you think he's being blackmailed over some woman?" I didn't feel in my bones this was the answer. Victor wouldn't mind a little scandal. He liked pretty women, and if the woman's husband didn't like it, it was the woman who'd be in a pickle, not Victor. "He'd never pay the kind of money we're talking about to a woman. He's interested in them, not insane."

"Actually it was music we were talking about," Sean reminded me.

"I don't get it."

"His violin is missing."

"So? Misplacing a violin isn't a crime. I wonder if he sold it, too—but surely not just before a concert."

"A violinist wouldn't do that unless he was planning to replace it with a better one. What would a really good violin cost—say one of those Stradivariuses you hear about."

I rolled my eyes to the ceiling in wonderment. "A fortune, if you could find one."

"Maybe that's what he bought then," he decided in his naiveté.

I shook my head. "I don't think so, Sean. They don't grow on trees, you know. If a Stradivarius had been for sale, the world would have heard about it. It would have been sold through Sotheby's or one of the international auction houses. When you consider that Stradivari has been dead for over two hundred years, and his output wasn't that high—well, you get the idea. They're like the works of the old masters painters—rare."

"How many would he have produced?" he persisted.

"I've heard Victor rant on about him occasionally. He said about eleven hundred or so instruments altogether, I think. He made violas and cellos as well, but fewer of them. And, of course, it was so long ago that about half of the instruments have been destroyed."

"Or lost. It's possible one of the five hundred and fifty odd ones gone missing has survived."

"Yes, but they can't just have 'survived' in some old shed. The wood would rot, and anyway they have to be played regularly or they lose their voice and die eventually."

"Violins don't die."

"Well, they fade away."

"You hear from time to time about a Stradivarius cropping up."

"It usually turns out to be something else—just an old violin that somebody has pasted a label in to con a gullible buyer. Victor wouldn't be fooled by that."

"Maybe he got hold of a genuine one," he insisted with a mulishness that was becoming tiresome.

"As I said, a genuine Stradivarius would be handled publicly through Sotheby's. And it would cost anywhere from a million up."

"If he planned to sell his apartment as well, he'd have a good down payment. Besides, Victor's an expert; he'd know the real

McCoy, whereas the guy trying to sell it to him wouldn't. It's possible he spotted one in some antique shop or . . ."

"Be real, Sean. If the store owner was holding Victor up for that kind of money, he'd have a pretty sharp idea he had a genuine Stradivarius on his hands, so why not get it authenticated and make his million? You know how high prices on rare paintings and things go when they're sold at public auction. The bidders get some kind of mass hysteria or something. A statue of a horse was sold for over ten million a while ago, and artists that are hardly known go for millions. No, it doesn't make any sense," I said and dismissed it.

His next idea was even worse. "Maybe it was stolen," he said, and shot me an apologetic glance. "That'd require some discretion—and a lot less than a million."

"What would be the point of buying a stolen violin? He couldn't play it in public. What you don't understand is that the existing Stradivarius violins are known. They have names and distinguishing characteristics, like people. The Library of Congress has one—it's called the Betts. There's another called the Swan, and one called the Cessol. The Musical Institute at Florence has the Tuscan—all well known, famous instruments. Stradivarius started out as a wood carver; he ornamented some of his violins. They weren't just churned out by a machine. They have people and animals and leaves and flowers and things on them. They're individual, very recognizable to people who are interested in such things."

He shrugged his big shoulders. "I saw a picture of one in the National Geographic. It didn't look any different from any other violin—no carvings. They can't all be as fancy as you're saying. A new Rembrandt turns up from time to time. I don't see why a Stradivarius couldn't, since he made over a thousand of them."

"It's not impossible," I relented, "but then it's within the realm of possibility that Victor was carried off by spacemen too. I think we'd be farther ahead to stick to the probable."

Sean's face turned pink, and when he spoke, his voice was slightly out of control. "I'm just trying to fit this grab-bag of unlikely facts together. There's a saying that when the impossible has been eliminated, what you're left with is the truth, however improbable."

"Then let's start by eliminating the impossible idea that Victor either knowingly bought a stolen violin or was dumb enough to buy one without knowing it was stolen."

"We've got a set of facts here that aren't going to go away just because you don't like them. Let's massage them a little and see what we come up with. One, Victor had a surprise, which he never got to reveal at the concert."

"That was my capriccio."

"You weren't so sure the night of the concert. Two, he was scraping together big bucks. Three, his own violin's disappeared."

"And four, Victor's disappeared. How does that fit into your scenario?"

"God, I hate that word 'scenario'. Okay, let's think about it. I don't know your uncle, but let's say he came across a Stradivarius and wanted to own it. He wouldn't tell anybody, especially the owner. Maybe the seller got such a good price out of him by pretending the thing was some other good make, like the one Victor owns—the Guan thing."

"Guarneri."

"There must be others as well."

"There's Amati—Stradivari studied under him. An Amati might be worth about the price Victor was accumulating," I admitted.

"So he buys it, not knowing it's a stolen Stradivarius."

"But he *would* know—I explained all that."

Sean exploded in a way that surprised me. I took him for a more gentle sort of a man, but his face turned reddish and he clenched his jaws and still couldn't stop himself from barking. "Christ, if there are five hundred and fifty of them in the world, he wouldn't know them *all* intimately."

I gave him a quelling stare. "Continue with your scenario."

"So he buys it, thinking he's made a great coup, then finds out it's hot."

"How does he suddenly find out?"

"He takes it to an expert."

"I guess that's what he'd do, all right."

"Who would that be—in Toronto, I mean?"

"He has a friend at the Royal Conservatory, a Dr. Bitwell, who's the country's top expert. All right, so Bitwell tells him he got stung. Then he'd go to the police," I said, with admirable restraint. "Or at least back to the man he bought it from."

"Do you think the guy would be dumb enough to still be there?"

"He wouldn't just run away and leave his antique shop."

"Maybe he doesn't have a shop. Maybe Victor just met him somewhere—at a party, or something."

"Oh really, Sean! This is becoming more ridiculous by the minute. This isn't Raymond Chandler; it's convoluted enough to be Hercule Poirot or Sherlock Holmes."

"Just hear me out, will you?" he asked stiffly. "We'll assume Bitwell told him the thing is stolen—he'd like to get his money back, but maybe he'd like even better just to keep the violin for himself. For a while anyway," he added quickly when I blasted him with a blistering glare. But I didn't interrupt verbally.

"Maybe he just wants to cuddle and play the thing for a day or so," Sean continued.

"Not at the price of a couple of hundred thousand bucks. He'd have gone straight to the police and reported it."

"Well, he didn't, so we can rule that out," Sean insisted.

"We can rule out this whole fabrication. You've OD'd on detective stories, Sean. You're hallucinating."

"I admit it's only a theory," he said defensively. "Of course, where it breaks down is when he learns the thing is stolen."

"It broke down long before that if you ask me. And you've left out the most important fact that Victor is missing." Something began fomenting in my head, which must have left some trace on my face as Sean was regarding me peculiarly.

"What is it?" he asked.

"That's why he was kidnapped!" I exclaimed, not a shout, but a shocked whisper. "Whoever he bought the damned thing from followed him and knew he was getting it authenticated when he went to the conservatory. He kept following him till he got the chance to steal the violin back, but Victor wouldn't give it up, so he had to steal my uncle too."

I stopped, waiting for Sean to tell me I was crazy. He sat, nodding in total agreement. "But when he kidnapped him, he found out he didn't have the violin, and he's been looking for it ever since!" The whole incident reeled around in my head, as sharp as though I were seeing it on the screen. The clues fell into place so neatly I forgot for the moment that the whole thing was founded on quicksand.

Sean seemed to follow this crabbed reasoning with no difficulty. "Exactly," he said, nodding his head. "What isn't quite so clear is where the violin got to."

"That's right, because if any of this is true, Victor must have had the violin he bought in the case when he went to see Dr. Bitwell."

"Bitwell!" Sean exclaimed triumphantly. "That's where Victor left it."

"The running shoes suggest he took the violin out at the Casa Loma."

"No, it only suggests he took an empty case into the Casa Loma. He left the Strad with Bitwell before he went to visit you. You've got to give Bitwell a call, Cassie."

But before I did, I wanted to rethink our mad story. How exactly had we got off on this track? It all began with Sean's idea that Victor had bought a stolen Stradivarius, and there was not one single shred of actual evidence that he'd done anything of the sort. I gently pointed this out to him, but it didn't budge him an iota.

"What's it going to cost to phone the guy?" he urged.

"If he had the violin, or even if Victor had been to see him, don't you think he would have called me, or the police? Or is he another of the covetous ones who wants to keep it for himself?"

"Hey, he could be! I never thought of that!" He smiled benignly on my brilliant inventiveness. "Or it could be that Bitwell's the one they've contacted about the ransom. I mean if they know he has the violin, and they would know if they made Victor talk . . ." He let it hang menacingly. Visions of a poor, tortured Victor rose up like something out of a horror movie.

"I'll make the call," I said. There was no answer at the conservatory, but Bitwell was in the phone book, so I called his house. There was no answer there either. "I'll call back tomorrow."

"First thing in the morning," he added, shaking a peremptory finger at me.

"I will call, because I'd feel guilty if I didn't, but I don't believe Bitwell will even know what I'm talking about. Victor was being blackmailed—that's what I think. I don't know what he did, but it makes more sense than thinking he's dumb enough to buy a stolen Stradivarius violin."

Sean relented into a smile. "It won't do any harm to call."

"Even if you're right, which you're not, it still doesn't account for the fact that my uncle's own del Gesù is missing. Where is it in all this tale? He was taking it to Roy Thomson Hall. That's what he had in that violin case that was suddenly full of my Adidas."

"He took the money in the case to buy the Stradivarius, and after he bought it, he put the Strad in the case," Sean explained patiently, as though to an idiot. "Or possibly he gave the del Gesù plus the money in exchange for the Stradivarius. The very fact that it's missing points that way. Yeah, that'd account for it." He appeared perfectly satisfied now, all the little ragged ends tucked into place.

"That violin was his wife. He wouldn't trade it in on a different one."

"I believe you mentioned your uncle is divorced?" I resisted the impulse to dash my coffee in his smug face.

"He wouldn't plan to play the Strad the very day he bought it. He'd want a few weeks to get used to the feel of it and work it into prime voice. He didn't sell the del Gesù the day of a big concert. And besides, whoever sold the Stradivarius to him must have known he'd want to have it authenticated. So why follow him and steal it back?"

"Maybe he didn't expect Victor to get it looked at so fast. If he'd waited a day or two, the guy that sold it to him would have had time to disappear. Why don't we hike over to that conservatory and see Bitwell in person tomorrow?" he suggested.

"Why not? It's your idea. You can share the ignominy of Bitwell's outrage when I suggest he'd been hiding a priceless instrument that doesn't belong to him."

"You'll feel different if he has it though, won't you?" he asked, trying to cajole me into a better mood.

"I'll feel nonplussed."

Sean set down his empty cup. "It's getting late."

"What time do you want to go to the conservatory tomorrow?"

"What time does it open?"

"Nine, I think."

"I'll pick you up at eight-thirty."

I got up to accompany him to the door. He took my hands in his and gave me an encouraging smile. I knew his story was foolishness, but I still appreciated that he was trying, in his goofy way, to help.

"I decided not to switch to the Park Plaza after all," he said. "It's a pretty ritzy place—charges a fortune. The Delta Inn's more my league."

"Is that where you're staying?"

He pulled out a key. I was becoming as sneaky as he was. I got a glimpse of the number while it dangled from his fingers. It was 327.

"Kind of lonesome, going back to an empty room," he said leadingly, sliding his hands up my arms till he grabbed me above the elbows.

This pass had to come sooner or later. If he'd been anyone else, it would have come sooner. Still, it was a long leap from not even having tried to kiss me to suddenly dropping a hint to stay overnight. I hadn't known Sean long in actual hours—just slightly more than one day, but we'd been together almost constantly and under such unusual circumstances that I felt I knew him fairly well. Well enough to know I could ease him out the door without much trouble.

"If you hurry, you'll have time to do something about it," I suggested, politely but firmly. "Try the bar."

"What, an old baldie like me? It takes a while for my brand of charm to work." A low chuckle trailed into my ear as his moustache attacked me. It felt a lot like steel wool or maybe more like a toothbrush. It was a very rough moustache.

Everything about that kiss was hard. His arms felt like the proverbial steel bands, his chest a barrel against me, solid as a tree trunk. I struggled for a few seconds, until I realized he wasn't going to give way without an undignified skirmish. Something had activated his libidinous instincts, and he drew one of my arms around him, while holding me tightly with the other.

Sean may have been made of steel and wood—I was only flesh and blood. The usual chemical reactions occurred. My heart fluttered to a faster beat and a warmish glow suffused me. After the battering my emotions had taken the past day, it felt good to have a man's arms around me, infinitely tender arms, too, despite their strength. Without quite knowing how I knew it, I knew Sean wouldn't persist if I were really unwilling. If I had simply said "no", he would have stopped, so I didn't say it.

My fingers were discovering interesting contours and textures of his back. There were bulges of hard muscle and valleys lined with bones, a gulley like a small canyon that was his spine. There was a flare of tendon out to shoulders bent around me.

We kissed with his bristly moustache tickling my upper lip, and I wondered in some corner of my brain if I could get used to the intrusion of so much hair into our kisses, or whether I should charm him into shaving it. Suddenly the moustache slipped from notice. It was his lips, tensing to a demanding firmness, and the emotions within me that took my full attention. Something inside me was melting away, leaving a puddle of warm butter where vital organs should be. The knees, too, were becoming wobbly. When Sean's fingers began a geographical exploration of their own, focusing more on the front of my anatomy than the back, I decided to quell the bonfire, before it got out of control.

I pulled away and looked at him, suddenly shy. Me, I mean. He didn't look shy at all. He looked hungry—not for food. His eyes devoured me.

"Thanks for everything, Sean," I said heartily, stepping back. He caught both hands and held them.

"You're welcome. I've got lots more to give whenever you're in a taking mood."

"How Shakespearean!" He didn't know when I was complimenting him and when I was giving the needle. He gave an uncertain look, unsure of my meaning. I kissed him on the nose and pulled back as he tried to slide his lips around to intercept it.

"I'm bushed. I'll see you at eight-thirty tomorrow. Come early if you like, and I'll scramble us some eggs."

He squeezed my fingers and had the self-control not to mention tonight's dinner and who had prepared it. "Eight?"

"Fine."

Another quick, fierce kiss and he was gone with a last reminder to lock the door. I felt very lonesome as I slid on the chain and rather frightened. I'd been entertaining the idea of asking him to stay on the sofa, but once you've kissed a man and explored his back, such an invitation would certainly be misunderstood, so I just hoped nobody came calling that night and went straight to bed. I set the alarm for seven, planning to tidy the kitchen and start breakfast before Sean arrived at eight.

My weary brain wanted something nice to think about in bed, so I thought of Sean and the kiss. Nice as it was, more important thoughts of Victor soon eased in to the back of my mind. Nothing had changed, yet suddenly here I was concentrating my attention on a Stradivarius violin that existed only in Sean's highly active imagination. I had promised to go to see Dr. Bitwell, which was patently a waste of time. I should be doing something more germane, though what that something was, I really had no idea.

I could talk to his friends, try to find out why Victor was being blackmailed. Nothing else could account for piling up cash. It was either blackmail, or he was planning a flight. Did he owe taxes? Now there was something to check up on tomorrow. Maybe he owed thousands of dollars, and planned to nip off instead of paying them. Having chiselled on his taxes was exactly the sort of thing Victor would do. I'd discuss it with Sean tomorrow, after Bitwell threw us out of his office.

CHAPTER 10

I know I set the alarm for seven. I have a very distinct memory of pinching my fingers on the little brass key that's too small to hold on to. It just failed, that's all. I awoke to the rattle of the front door being kicked, while shouts and profanities roared through it.

I leapt a foot from bed and ran to peek out the little hole. Sean looked fit to be tied. His western hat was all askew, and he held some brown bags in his arms, which explained why he was kicking the door rather than beating it. He was with the doorman, who at that very moment was unlocking the door with his master key. The chain was all that kept them both from a view of me in nothing but a short nightie.

"Wait!" I hollered. "Let me get a housecoat."

"Cassie, are you all right?" Sean shouted.

"I'm fine."

There were apologetic mutters to the doorman, and when I got back with a housecoat on, there was a man who didn't know whether he was more embarrassed or angry or grateful.

"I'm terribly sorry, Sean. I set the alarm for seven, but it didn't go off."

Then the damned thing decided to work. A keening, brazen ringgggg went on and on till I ran into the bedroom to silence it. When I turned back to the bedroom door, Sean was there, arms akimbo, perusing my legs. He had finally decided on his feeling. He was smiling, albeit reluctantly, at the fact that I had miscalculated and set the alarm for eight.

"You scared the hell out of me," he said. "I was sure you'd disappeared too. I had to convince Hans—that's the doorman—that you were dead, and convinced myself into the bargain."

"Wishful thinking."

His eyes continued to leisurely exploration of what the housecoat revealed, and concealed, for that matter. "That's not my wishful thought at this very moment," he parried.

"I'm dying for some coffee, too," I said and smiled annoyingly.

"Did you know Hans has keys to all the doors?" he asked.

"He's bonded and researched and all sorts of things. A regular Caesar's wife. Besides, he's a big fan of Victor's." Although I talked about Hans, what I was really noticing was the glow of concern, or love, that was beating down on me when Sean said I'd scared the hell out of him. It was practically a declaration of love; I felt warm and shining all over.

"I look ghastly. Give me a minute to pull myself together." I brushed the tousled hair out of my face, and yanked my housecoat belt more tightly around me.

"You're wrong; you look great," he said, still glowing.

"Considering that you were expecting to see a corpse."

"You look just the way I thought you'd look in the morning. I'll put on water."

"No!" I shouted, so fiercely that he jumped. "I haven't cleaned up the kitchen. I went straight to bed last night. Oh, darn it, I wanted to have everything nice."

He lunged forward and put an arm around me to pull me against his hip. "You're safe, and that's pretty nice for starters after the scare you gave me. Go on, make yourself decent while I start on the kitchen. I'll just pretend I'm your husband. I'll scramble you some eggs."

My vitals were melting again. Where had this paragon come from? "How'd you know I like my eggs scrambled?"

"Alimentary, my dear Watson."

"Sheer luck, Holmes."

"No, you said last night you'd scramble me some. I noticed you only had one left, so I brought a dozen and some Canadian bacon. We were getting low on cream too. I switched us to half and half. Less calories for you."

"We women should take up a collection and have you cloned."

"I kind of like being unique," he smiled, "as long as I'm appreciated." Emboldened by my praise, he risked a pat on my hind quarters before he left.

I had a two-minute shower and hurried into my second best cotton dress, a black and white striped affair that Victor calls my zebra dress. Actually it's quite cute, a wraparound with big patch pockets in the front. By the time I got my damp hair pulled into a chignon and put a smear of makeup on, I could smell the bacon. The aroma was driving me crazy.

"You're a doll," I said to reward him. Sean had cleared the table and stacked the dishwasher, too, so I kissed him on the ear.

"Save those goodies for when the toast isn't going up in smoke. That doesn't mean don't do it. Just don't do it now," he said over his shoulder.

He looked very much at home in a kitchen, pulling the toast out while stirring the eggs with his other hand. He moved with the precise, smooth motions of a trained cook. I scanned his preparations and couldn't find anything to do but pour orange juice and put the cream on the table. While he finished the eggs, timed to be done when the bacon was ready, I poured the coffee.

"These eggs are so nice and fluffy!" I complimented between gobbles. "And the bacon is lovely too. Where'd you learn to cook?"

"I do most of my own cooking. You get tired of eating out."

"I thought you lived with your mother!"

"What made you think that? I'm thirty-one years old, Cassie. A bit long in the tooth to be living with Momma." A glint in his eye told me this was a crack at Ronald. "You know, before we set out for the conservatory, maybe you should give Bitwell a call at home. He might not get to work till eleven or some damned thing."

"We should check the mail on the way out, too, in case Victor sent himself anything else."

While I cleared the table and did the kitchen, Sean took the key down to get the mail. It was a good thing I phoned Bitwell. He was starting his holidays and going to Muskoka that

morning, but he wanted to see me before he left. The note of
concern in his voice gave rise to a hope, or fear, that he had
something to tell us. As he was in a hurry to get away, I ran
downstairs and met Sean. He had a few envelopes in his hand,
mostly bills, and one letter from Victor's stockbroker.

I opened the letter while Sean drove us to Bitwell's
apartment on University Avenue, north of Bloor.

"Maybe he got a hot tip on some stock. Maybe that's why he
borrowed all that money," I said hopefully. "Ronald probably
gave him some inside info—he works in that line, you know."

"Open it," he said laconically. I thought he was unhappy
with my reference to Ronald.

What Victor had done was sell every stock he owned.
Apparently he had already gotten the check; what I held in my
hand was the month-end statement listing the sales and prices.
It came to over fifteen thousand dollars.

"I wonder how much he accumulated altogether," Sean said,
frowning into the sun. His western hat was on the seat beside
him.

"He hasn't actually got any money from the cottage yet.
And he only got a deposit on the car. Of course he has the loan
from the bank and his advance from the concert along with this
money."

We mulled this over till we reached Bitwell's place. Bitwell
was a widower who lived alone in a one bedroom apartment
that had the uncared-for air of a womanless home. The
furnishings were tired looking without actually being shabby.
He had the same unloved look himself. A wife would have
nagged him into losing that pot and getting his hair cut. She
would have bought a less garish shirt than the red and white
one he wore for beginning his holidays, too.

"As I told you, I'm just on my way back to the cottage," he
explained, with a deprecating gesture at the shirt. "School lets
out this week, and my daughter's sending the grandchildren up
for a visit. I went up Wednesday evening and opened the place.
Thank God I didn't have any vandalism—just some squirrels
that got in and made a mess in the living room."

Lonesome—he babbled like a lonesome man. He showed us
to a seat while he talked, and sat down himself. He seemed
apologetic. "I would have called you sooner, Miss Newton, if

I'd had any idea of all this commotion. I don't have a TV at the cottage and didn't have the radio on—they play nothing but trash. I didn't know your uncle had disappeared till I glanced at the papers this morning. I meant to call you. I only got back late last night. I'm very sorry, and if there's anything I can do, be sure to get in touch. I have a phone at the cottage."

"There's probably nothing you can do," I began, "but I was just wondering if you'd heard from my uncle before he disappeared. I'm trying to contact anyone he might have talked to that day, you know, and as you're one of his friends . . ."

"I did! That's why I was going to phone you or drop around to the apartment this morning before I left. He called on me at work Wednesday afternoon, about four o'clock. I was just about to leave."

And my heart was about to jump out of my mouth. "What did he say—what did he do?"

His eyes glowed with a light that sent my nerves into convulsions. "He had the violin with him," he said, nodding wisely. "I saw no mention of it in the papers. What happened to the Stradivarius?"

I stared at him, then turned to stare at Sean. You never saw such a satisfied smile on any man who hadn't just won the Irish Sweepstakes. "That's what we're trying to find out," Sean said. "We were hoping he'd left it with you."

"No, no. He'd hardly let me touch it, though he played it for me. The little capriccio he wrote for you, Miss Newton. A pretty air. The instrument was in good voice, with potential for greatness. Someone took excellent care of it over all the years. He wanted me to authenticate it for him. It was a genuine Stradivarius, of course—not one of the highly ornamented ones. There's no mistaking a Stradivarius. His varnish is still a mystery to us after all these years—centuries. It had the soft, rich, mature appearance—nothing but age imparts that glow to the varnish. And there was that symmetry of the head, the exquisite design of the *f* holes. But you aren't interested in that!" he said, drawing himself back from his reverie. "I put its date as Stradivari's golden period—somewhere in the early seventeen hundreds. The back was in one piece, you see, so it came after his Amatisé models. Not a Long Pattern. I recognized it at once. It quite took the wind out of his sails." He shook his head in sorry commiseration.

Not once during the speech did Sean so much as glance at me. I kept looking at him, trying to catch his eye, but he was staring at Bitwell the way a hunter cat stares at its prey. A quick, puzzled look flitted over his rugged features then subsided to a look of satisfaction.

"Why would your authenticating it take the wind out of his sails?" I asked. It seemed exactly the wrong reaction.

"He was hoping it was a new discovery. To learn he'd paid a hundred and seventy-five thousand for a well-known, stolen violin didn't sit will, as you may imagine."

"Stolen!" I gasped.

"Undoubtedly. It was the one stolen from the Contessa Carpani around the New Year. She had a robbery at her villa in Italy, some jewels were taken as well. It wasn't given as much publicity as you might think. I expect she didn't want to broadcast what other items she had, in case of another robbery. I was alerted by the Mounted Police, as a precaution only, in case it was brought to me for authentication. These thefts where the spoils are sold internationally are handled by Interpol," he said. His red and white shirt expanded in pride at being connected with such sophisticated goings on.

"The only ornamentation on it was a small cluster of grapes and leaves, inlaid in ebony around the sound holes," he continued. "It had never been displayed or lent out to exhibitions, so it isn't a well known instrument like the Betts or Alard. I was very surprised Victor wasn't familiar with the violin, though, as he had been visiting Italy quite near the Carpanis' villa a few years ago, but it seemed he never managed an introduction and so hadn't seen the violin. He didn't even know it was missing."

"Where in Italy was Mr. Mazzini visiting?" Sean asked.

"Why, near the Carpanis' villa, as I said," Dr. Bitwell repeated.

"Where's that?"

"Not far from Cremona, where Stradivari created his instruments," Bitwell told him.

"Victor comes from Milan! That's where he was, visiting his

relatives! It's close to Cremona," I said hastily. Next thing I knew, Sean would be saying my uncle had arranged the heist from the Contessa's villa himself.

"Wouldn't the price, only a hundred and seventy-five thousand, give Mazzini a hint the thing was stolen?" Sean asked.

"Ah no, he had no idea," Bitwell said, with admirable firmness. "Not all Stradivari's works sell for a million. He met the seller, an English chap, by chance at a party. Etherington, his name was. He got chatting to Victor about violins and mentioned a very fine instrument in his possession. He said he bought it for a hundred dollars in Dorset twenty years before and thought at the time he had a precious instrument, but he didn't actually know much about violins, though he was an ardent amateur. He never bothered having it looked at by an expert. When he came to Canada ten years ago, he brought it along and still had it. Victor arranged to have a look at it, and made the tactical error of claiming it was a Stradivarius. Etherington was delighted, and of course the price shot up to the stars. Victor said he could have got it for a thousand dollars if he'd kept his mouth shut, but then he never is able to do that," he admitted sadly.

"Why didn't Etherington get it evaluated himself?" I asked.

"Because he didn't believe for a minute it could be a Stradivarius, is what Victor thought," Bitwell answered swiftly. "And Victor knew perfectly well it was, and knew he'd pay more than a hundred and seventy-five thousand for it at auction. Of course Etherington knew it *was* genuine, and knew it was stolen, too, but he let on he was just a semi-ignorant type. Each of them was trying to hoodwink the other is what it comes down to, but it was Victor who got fleeced in the end." Dr. Bitwell was a big enough man that he really felt sorry and not jubilant.

"What did my uncle do when you told him it was stolen?" I asked.

"He put it back in its case."

"His own case or a different one?" Sean asked.

"It was the case he carries his del Gesù in. I told him he had to go at once to the police, but he said no, he'd find Etherington first and blacken both his eyes. He couldn't even stop payment on the check, since he'd paid cash. Such a foolish thing to do, but Etherington told him he wanted to keep it off the record for tax purposes, you see, which made the kind of larcenous sense Victor understands. And it saved himself the percent sales tax as well."

I scanned the events and times and said, "He came to see me at the Casa Loma before five, so he obviously didn't contact Etherington. He must have realized by then that Etherington was following him. Do you know where Etherington lived or worked?"

Dr. Bitwell shook his head. "He didn't say, but Victor must have known. I'm sure they didn't meet on a street corner to do business. He should have gone directly to the police, but he has a sort of fondness for rogues, you know. He didn't want to throw Etherington into the arms of the law. Or maybe he was trying to figure out some means of keeping the violin, for a while at least. I wouldn't be surprised if he planned to get his money back from Etherington and keep the violin till it could be returned to the Contessa in Italy."

"Maybe he wanted to keep it for this series of concerts," Sean mentioned.

"No," Bitwell said, "Etherington asked him if he meant to use it for the concert series. He was too much of an amateur to realize Victor would have wanted to have it adjusted perfectly and practice on it for a few weeks."

"What did Victor tell him?" Sean asked.

"He told him he wouldn't use it. In fact, Victor asked Etherington not to mention the sale at all. He wanted to get it in voice then call in the press and play something for them. Victor understands self-promotion."

Sean and I exchanged a telling look. So that was why Etherington tried to steal the violin back—because my uncle was taking it straight to have it authenticated, and once he learned it was stolen, there would be free advertising aplenty. Headlines galore and Etherington still in town.

"I imagine Victor hoped to buy it from the Contessa," Bitwell continued. "If she'd ever sell to anyone, it would be to someone like the Great Mazzini. You should have seen how lovingly he handled it, running his fingers over the magical varnish, fondling it like a lover," he finished with a wistful smile. Then added less wistfully, "He wouldn't let me play a note."

I felt there were dozens of things I should be asking Dr. Bitwell, but they refused to fall into place. It was Sean who spoke up.

"Did Victor think anyone was following him?"

"He didn't say so. I didn't think to look after him when he left."

"Why would Etherington follow him anyway?" I asked.

"Just to make sure the Carpani Strad didn't become public knowledge too soon," Sean suggested.

"He need not have worried," Bitwell said. "The grand gesture, the shocking surprise—that's Mazzini's way."

Sean nodded. "Do you know where he originally met Etherington, where the party took place? Was it a private house?"

"I have no idea. All we talked about was the violin. I read Victor a lecture on his foolishness, and that made him angry with me."

"I wonder what he did with his own violin, his del Gesù," I said. "Did he mention that to you?"

Bitwell gave a frowning pause. "I had the impression it was at his apartment, but I don't remember that he actually said so. He told me the Strad didn't come with a case. Etherington had it wrapped in a towel, inside a plastic bag, so he took his empty case to carry it home. I assumed he'd left his own violin at home. What else would he have done with it? He'd never leave it in his car, unattended."

"He bought this violin on Wednesday, did he?" Sean verified.

"Late Wednesday afternoon," Bitwell confirmed. "He brought it straight to me. The label had fallen off and was loose inside the instrument. He shook it out, and saw it was indeed a Stradivarius. The label is quite unmistakable. Stradivari had a wooden date stamp that he used. It said 'Antonius Stradivarius Cremonenfis Faciebat Anno 1,' and he filled the date in by hand. The last numbers were unclear—I thought it said 1707, but Victor wasn't sure it wasn't 1701. There was the little symbol in the lower right corner as well, a cross with his initials beneath, enclosed in a circle. Quite unmistakable. The

Carpani Strad is known to have been dated 1707, which is perhaps why Victor insisted the date read 1701. It was a very good time for Stradivari, his Golden Period."

Dr. Bitwell was glancing at his watch. "If there's nothing else, I'm supposed to pick up the children at ten," he said politely.

"What's that number in Muskoka where you can be reached?" Sean asked, and wrote the number down. "The police may want to be in touch with you."

"I'm going to contact them before I leave. I should have phoned earlier, but it seemed more—kind to talk to you first, Miss Newton. I hope your uncle is found soon. You needn't worry about his safety. Etherington is a rogue, but that's not to say he'd murder. That's a much more serious business. He wouldn't do that only for a pile of money," he assured me.

We thanked this naive optimist and left. Intriguing as the interview had been, I was more intrigued to discover how Sean knew all this had happened before we talked to Bitwell. He had outlined roughly the whole scene last night. Just pulled it out of thin air, so to speak. Obviously he knew more than a hardware merchant on holiday from Nebraska had any reason to know, and my next step was to discover who he really was.

He wore a cocky smile as we went to the car. "What did I tell you?" he crowed.

I got in and folded my skirt around me. "Strangely enough, you told me so. Now how's about telling me how you knew so much?"

"Deduction," he said, tapping his temple.

"Bullshit! Who are you anyway, and what's your interest in Victor?"

He stared with a look of surprise that went beyond merely corrugating his forehead. Blank amazement was in his eyes, and he let his mouth fall open. "What are you talking about? We worked it out together last night. You had as much to do with figuring it out as I did."

"Oh no, I can't take credit for dredging up the idea of a Stradivarius violin—a stolen one at that! That's a little too pat, Sean. You weren't at the Casa Loma by chance, and you didn't make a pass at me because you liked my fat body."

"Boney, I'd call it."

Flattery got him nowhere. "You saw Victor with me, and figured I was somebody who knew him well—that's why you hit on me. So who are you? A policeman, a friend of Mr. Etherington, perhaps?" I suggested. I was only being ironical, though the words had hardly left my mouth before I realized the distinct possibility of this last-named identity. God, he could *be* Etherington for all I knew. His accent had a way of sliding around from the midwest to Texas, though it had never veered toward England yet.

Victor had gotten away with the Strad, which he quickly discovered was stolen. Etherington hadn't counted on that. But what had then led him to kidnap my uncle instead of running for the hills? There had to be another piece to this puzzle. Had he planned all along to get rid of Victor? Did he make a career of selling that violin then stealing it back and killing the buyer?

All these unlikely possibilities flitted through my mind in seconds. "Be real," was Sean's disarming reply. "If Mr. deBeers vanished, wouldn't you think maybe diamonds had something to do with it?"

"Yes, and if it were Antonio Stradivari who vanished, I might go along with that analogy."

"Just hear me out," he said. "And if it turned out deBeers had been lumping together a batch of money, wouldn't you think maybe it was diamonds he meant to buy? So a famous violinist disappears, also his violin, and it's staring you in the face. It has something to do with a violin. When you think expensive violin, you think Stradivarius. When the whole thing is done in a clandestine way, paying cash, the possibility pops up that there was something fishy about the deal. That's all—simple deduction."

"That's about as simple as the theory of relativity."

"Whatever," he shrugged his shoulders and pulled into the line of traffic.

It was his innocent looks that made me doubt he was personally involved. I couldn't decide whether he was an idiot who just happened to hit on the truth, or whether he'd been guiding my thoughts. He'd certainly been guiding my actions and with a very heavy hand. He had insisted we go to Bitwell, but why drag me there unless he wanted me to learn the truth? And Bitwell *was* telling the truth—that I refused to doubt.

The staunch profile hunched over the wheel told me nothing. "Where to next?" he asked, with his usual disregard for the finer points of grammar.

"Home, James." I closed my eyes against the sun and distraction of traffic to think.

CHAPTER 11

It wasn't easy to get rid of Sean when we drove into the parking garage of the apartment building.

"There are all kinds of things we should be doing," he insisted, not knowing that what I planned to do was follow him and try to find out who and what he was.

"You're right. I haven't washed my hair in days. Since I gave the housekeeper a few days off, I should haul out the vacuum and clean up the apartment, too."

He was amazed at my sudden descent into domesticity. "I mean about finding the violin."

"Bitwell said he'd call the police. I'll probably be hearing from them soon, and it's my uncle *I'm* looking for. Apparently you have other priorities."

Angry that he'd finally slipped up on some detail, Sean let off a string of oaths, containing in their midst the notion that the violin would lead to Victor—all we had to do was find the del Gesù. "If we did a little brainstorming, we'd come up with something."

"It's not in the apartment, and it wasn't in his car. He must have stashed it in a locker, too."

"Then we'll look for the key," he decided, and smiled triumphantly. "How long will all this cleaning up take you?"

"A couple of hours."

"I'll go through his pockets while you work."

"He doesn't have two hours worth of pockets."

We both knew that if there were a locker key, it was in the suit Victor wore, but I didn't want to make him too suspicious, and I didn't want to lose track of him entirely, either. If he left now he'd be on his way before I could get up to Bloor Street and grab a cab to follow him. I'd have to postpone the cleaning up, but I'd let him come up and we'd go through my uncle's pockets.

"All right. We left half a pot of coffee. We might as well finish it."

I turned on the coffee, but we didn't get around to drinking it. There was no key in Victor's pockets, and just as Sean was offering to wield the vacuum while I washed by hair, Eleanor Strathroy landed in on us. She looked distinctly alarmed to see a strange man with me.

Eleanor is a black-eyed, black-haired, usually black-gowned and I suspected black-hearted little woman of extreme elegance. She must be in the vicinity of fifty, but she could pass for ten years younger, except for the eyes. The figure is well under control, the skin oiled to a youthful bloom, but the eyes lack the luster of youth. Her pupils are two sharp little pinpricks of black. One of her major concerns in life is guarding her face and figure. I usually met her with Victor and didn't think I'd be comfortable alone with her. As far as she was concerned, we two women were alone.

She hardly looked at Sean when I introduced him as a friend from the States. Friends who wore faded jeans and boots during a working day were invisible. The black dress she wore today was linen, severely tailored with a white, pointed collar. Joan Crawford would have looked right at home in it. She wore jet black earrings and beads and a Cartier tank watch.

"Would you like some coffee, Eleanor? I've just heated some up," I offered.

"Slow poison," she said, dismissing it with a wave of her hand. "Cassie, where have you been at this hour of the morning? Ronald dropped in on his way to the office and was worried sick when you weren't here. Since he called me, I've been phoning and phoning. I finally decided to come over and see if you were all right."

"I've only been gone an hour!"

"You didn't call yesterday. You said you'd keep in touch," she accused.

"I said I'd let you know if I learned anything."

"You haven't heard from Victor then?" she asked, her eyes imploring me to give good news. I was suddenly taken with the idea that she intended to marry my uncle. I'd always thought of their relationship as a light, lascivious friendship, but she looked genuinely worried.

"No, I'm afraid not."

"He's dead. He must be dead," she sighed, tears springing to her eyes as she rifled in her black Gucci bag for a handkerchief. I was surprised to see a plain old Kleenex clutched in her fingers when they came out.

I tried to calm her, though I was a basket of nerves myself. "There's no reason to think that, Eleanor. I spoke to Dr. Bitwell this morning. You know Dr. Bitwell, from the conservatory."

She frowned, shaking her head. "I don't believe I do."

"You met him here." Her memory wasn't too good for old tweed jackets with patched elbows. A symphony conductor, an artist or an opera singer she would have recalled with ease. Bitwell was only known to a handful of experts, so she had forgotten him.

"Of course, Bitwell," she said vaguely.

I revived her memory and related the story of Victor and the Stradivarius.

"That's shocking!" she exclaimed. "But if Etherington knew the thing was a Stradivarius, and stolen to boot, he must have known Victor would produce it in public at the first opportunity, so why . . ."

I explained that Etherington had checked this and been assured by my uncle that he didn't mean to produce the Strad immediately. "But Etherington's had plenty of time to leave the country by now," I concluded, "and still no Victor."

As Sean had been totally ignored during our talk, I looked a question at him. "It seems logical," he said slowly. "On the other hand, he took payment in Canadian currency. You wouldn't think he'd run off to a foreign country with a case full of Canadian bills. It'd be a problem to get them exchanged. A bank might ask questions, and if he used the black market, he'd lose a good percentage. It would make more sense to deposit the money in a bank—or better, a couple of banks—and arrange a transfer, or travellers' checks. That'd take a little while. I imagine all Etherington wanted was enough time to get that money into a more convenient form, but when Victor headed straight to Bitwell, he was afraid he wouldn't have time to do it."

Any lingering doubt that Sean was a dumb hick had to be forgotten. My doubts had come back when he offered to vacuum. He was quicker than Eleanor and me together to pick up on these fine points. I don't claim to be a financial genius, but Eleanor is no slouch.

"But surely in a country the size of Canada this Etherington could have hidden out somewhere," she said doubtfully. "He certainly had no shortage of money."

"He wouldn't know whether Victor kept track of the serial numbers. He might have," Sean suggested. Sean was rapidly rising from dumb hick to policeman. Or could it be all his detective reading that made him think of marked bills? "Even if the bills weren't marked, the serial numbers might have been listed."

"So complicated," Eleanor mused.

"Of course another possibility is that Etherington was just a go-between for someone else. His instructions might have been to follow Victor and see where he went," Sean explained.

"Or his instructions might have been to steal the violin back once he got the money," I threw in. "Maybe it wasn't the plan for anyone else ever to see the violin, but my uncle got away from them somehow. Victor's no fool. He wouldn't meet Etherington in a dark alley at night. He'd arrange the sale for a public place, in daylight."

"How do you know the violin was stolen?" Eleanor asked, looking from Sean to me as she spoke.

"Dr. Bitwell recognized it. It was stolen from a Contessa near Cremona in Italy," I explained.

Eleanor looked as though I'd just announced the end of the world. She struggled for breath, then shrieked, "Surely not Contessa Carpani's Stradivarius!"

Sean's head slued around so hard I thought he'd give himself a whiplash. "Do you know her?" he barked.

"I met her—oh, a couple of years ago! It was the summer I met Victor, but I didn't meet him at the Contessa's villa. I met him in Milan. My sister, Signora Crispi, is acquainted with the Contessa. We were invited to dinner at the Villa Carpani. I was sorry Victor had already left; he would have loved a chance to see the violin."

"This was when your husband was alive, was it?" Sean asked. "Since you said 'we' were invited."

"No, no, Harold has been dead longer. Ronald and I were visiting the Crispis. I believe I will have a cup of that coffee, Cassie. Black, no sugar." I got it, and she took a sustaining sip while the color seeped back into her face.

"I suppose you told Victor all about the violin—the unusual oramentation on the front. Grapes and leaves, inlaid in ebony," Sean said.

He was fishing to see if Victor knew he was buying a stolen violin, but as he didn't look at me, he missed my glare.

"Did it have grapes on it? So long ago," she said, waving her hand. "I really don't remember. I may have told him."

Sean's frustration was obvious, but no matter how many times he repeated the question, Eleanor couldn't remember describing the violin to Victor. She didn't know much about violins. She had only bothered to have a look at it because it was a Stradivarius. She liked famous names.

"Where did the contessa keep it?" he asked.

"In the music room at her villa. No particular precautions were taken. Of course the villa is full of treasures, and the house has an alarm system, to say nothing of the staff of servants. You'll find it was one of them who took it. It's odd Audrey didn't tell me of the Contessa's loss. When did it happen?"

"Around New Year's," I told her.

"Who's Audrey, your sister?" Sean asked.

Eleanor sipped more coffee and nodded. A frown creased her well-tended brow but not for long. She reached and smoothed away its last traces with her fingers. "I was out of town at New Year's; that would explain my not hearing about the contessa's loss. Ron and I were skiing at Mont Tremblant. I must be running along to an appointment now. I just popped in to see that you're all right, Cassie."

"Time for me to be shoving off, too," Sean said. "I'll call you around noon, Cassie. Can I drop you somewhere, Mrs. Strathroy?"

I was glad to be rid of him, but a little surprised at his offer to give Eleanor a lift. Eleanor was more than shocked; she was offended. "I have my car," she said haughtily. "Ronald will call you, dear." She gave me a frosty peck on the cheek, and allowed Sean to hold the front door and lead her to the elevator. I had a feeling she wouldn't exchange a word with him all the way down, and that Sean would chat away despite her silence. He'd obviously gone with her to see what else he could discover about the Contessa Carpani. What he was trying to find out was whether Victor knew he was buying a stolen violin, or maybe whether he'd arranged to steal it himself. I knew Victor hadn't been in Italy around the New Year; he was playing a series of concerts in New York at the time.

My plan was to follow Sean, and as soon as the elevator door closed, I grabbed my purse and hurried out to take the next one down. If he took his car, he'd have to go to the service elevator, so I might follow him as he drove out, if I had the luck to catch a cab immediately. I waited impatiently, watching the numbers change as the elevator came up. It stopped at floor seventeen, the door opened, and a short man of swarthy complexion got out. With my nerves already jumping, I felt frightened by the way he stared at me, but he just brushed past without saying anything. The door was gliding shut behind me when I recognized him—or his suit. Surely that was the same rumpled blue polyester suit, shiny as plastic, and the same man inside it, who had been at the Casa Loma the day my uncle disappeared!

Panic grew inside me as the elevator went quietly down. I punched the button, and got out at floor fifteen, not knowing what I was going to do, but knowing I couldn't let this chance pass. I had to do something. I'd go back up to the seventeenth floor and at least spy on the man, see where he was going. Could he possibly be going anywhere else but to my apartment? I used the stairs, as the elevator had already left, and besides I wanted to sneak up quietly on the man in the blue suit.

The stairs were blocked off by the required fire-safe door. I opened the door an inch and peeked down the hall, toward Victor's apartment. The man was there all right, but it wasn't Victor's door he was at. It was Betty Friske's, and she was just letting him in.

A million questions spewed into my head, foremost among them the usual one—what should I do? What *could* I do? I could wait for the man to come out and follow him, or I could follow Sean if I moved fast. The little swarthy man was a peripheral figure in my mystery, so I opted to follow Sean and took the elevator from floor sixteen. I stood in front of the apartment building, looking up and down for the silver Monte Carol. I didn't see it, but before long I spotted Sean on foot, dodging along at a fast clip but always making sure to stay behind another pedestrian. He was tailing somebody!

I fell in behind him, doing the same thing. Before long, I realized it was Eleanor he was following. Her black dress and his big hat made them easy to see. Now why in hell was he doing this? At times he did behave like a boy, playing detective. Eleanor trotted briskly along to the Hazelton Lanes Mall. When she went into a shop, Sean strolled along a bit and waited. I waited still farther behind him. Eleanor's "appointment" was just a shopping spree. She went from store to store for nearly an hour, and Sean dogged her every step. When she left, she went back to the parking garage at our apartment building, and Sean followed her.

I followed him by cab when his rented Monte Carlo nosed around the corner, hot on the trail of Eleanor's aged but still shiny Lincoln. She went to Ronald's office on Bay Street. I got out a block later and doubled back. I thought Sean would show up sooner or later, but I'd lost him. Maybe he spotted me following him. Since I wasn't the least interested in Eleanor's itinerary, I took a taxi home, as nervous as ever when the elevator door pulled open at floor seventeen. There was no little blue-suited man there waiting for me. Still with Betty Friske, getting his face bruised, no doubt.

If he was, they were being quiet about it. Not a sound came through the adjoining wall. A little later, Betty's door opened and she came out alone, dressed up for a day touring the stores or beauty parlors. The peacock blue suit looked hideous with her orange hair. She looked like a cheap actress or high class waitress. She didn't look as if she belonged in our building at all. What could the little man have to do with Betty? And more importantly, had he been with Sean at the Casa Loma, as I had first thought that day that now seemed so long ago?

Coincidence is known for its long arm, but it would have to be elastic for that man to happen to be at the Casa Loma around the time of my uncle's disappearance, standing right beside Sean, and now turn up snooping around next door, and for him not to be involved. Was he an associate of Sean's, and was Betty one of them as well? Sean had been quick to volunteer to talk to her. As I thought it over, it seemed less likely she and Sean could have fallen into each other's arms so easily with no former acquaintance.

Betty was a friend of my uncle's. She could have fingered him as a likely buyer for the stolen Strad if they were all working together. Was I nuts? I was fast heading in that direction with so much confusion.

I tried diligently to marshall facts, suspicions and suspects into rows on a piece of paper, but nothing matched. Sean's sitting on my tail was more than coincidence, but why did he lead me by the nose to discover things he'd be better off without my knowing? And there was still Etherington to consider. Was he Sean? I was suspicious that Sean, who remembered so many details, hadn't thought to ask what Etherington looked like. An Englishman was the only way Bitwell had described him. Anybody using an English accent would be taken for an Englishman at first acquaintance. Anybody could say he was from Dorset, just like anyone could say he was from North Platte.

I checked the atlas, and North Platte was there on the Platte River, just where Sean said it was. Not that that proved anything except that Sean had an atlas. I decided to phone Dr. Bitwell and get Etherington's description. It was Sean who had gotten his number, but Bitwell was in the Muskoka directory, and the operator gave me the number.

He hadn't arrived yet when I first called, but the second time, he answered. "Did you remember to call the police?" I asked him.

"Yes, I did. I gave them the information before I left Toronto. They were very grateful. Have you heard anything?"

I said no, and asked him about Etherington's appearance.

"Victor didn't say much about his looks. Only that he was an Englishman. He said he had a moustache, and wore tinted glasses—not sunglasses, but regular glasses with a little tint. He wondered later if they were a disguise, but he didn't seem to think so at first. Sorry I can't be of more help."

"Wait—don't hang up. Did he say anything about his size, or what he was wearing, his hair coloring, birthmarks?"

"Nothing like that, except he said the man was well-dressed, I believe. Yes, now I look back on it, he said something about 'an old school tie sort of English bloke.' I don't know whether he meant it literally about the tie or just meant that type of Englishman."

A stereotype, a sort of broad caricature, to emphasize the nationality. That's what Etherington sounded like to me. I thanked Bitwell and hung up. The little swarthy man couldn't be Etherington. The first thing anyone would have mentioned about him was his size. He didn't wear a moustache, not that he couldn't have stuck one on for the occasion, but Sean actually wore one, and he did accents too. He might own a jacket that would lead Victor, the clothes horse, to call him well dressed. He'd kept it off his back if he owned one, but it was possible.

As I considered it, Sean's whole western persona was rather broadly drawn, more of a caricature than anything else. Easy to describe, like Etherington, and even easier to change. Just pull off the hat and boots and jeans, and cut the twang from his voice. I was sorry I hadn't stayed on his tail when he stopped at Bay Street. And why on earth was he doing that? This strange mixture of idiocy and wily intelligence baffled me. He should have shaved off the moustache if he was Etherington. And he had led me to discover Etherington himself—curiouser and curiouser.

It wasn't quite noon yet, but when the phone peeled, I felt a sinking, sad and certain feeling it was Sean. It was a relief to hear Ronald's voice.

"I've just heard from Mom, Cassie," he said.

"About Dr. Bitwell?"

"Yes, that's an unexpected turn! A Stradivarius violin. It's starting to sound like a vulgar melodrama."

The Strathroys would hate vulgar melodrama worse than they hated polyester. "A stolen Stradivarius at that. Stolen from a neighbor of your sister, isn't that a coincidence?" I said. "Your mother knows the Contessa Carpani."

"The strangest thing of all is that Victor didn't recognize the violin," he replied. There was a tinge of insinuation in his voice.

"How could he recognize something he'd never seen?"

"That cluster of grapes should have distinguished it. I'm sure Mom must have described the thing to him in detail. However, that's neither here nor there; I'm not suggesting your uncle is criminally involved. I called to see if you're free for lunch."

I had taken offense on my uncle's behalf, and said very curtly, "I already have plans, thanks anyway."

"With the American you went to the concert with?" he asked stiffly.

"That's the one."

"Have you been seeing a lot of him?" he asked. An edge of jealously was definitely creeping into his voice now, and I gave it a shove.

"Practically all of him."

"I beg your pardon?" A joke is wasted on the Strathroys, which is one of the things I find off-putting about them.

"A fair bit," I translated. "He doesn't know anyone else in town."

"He didn't have any trouble picking you up. You'd think he'd have the common courtesy to leave you alone at a time like this." He was trying to hide his jealousy beneath a veneer of concern, but the rebuke was intended for me all the same. I didn't even have the excuse of saying the Strathroys had abandoned me. They'd been hounding me incessantly.

"He's helped me a lot," was my only defense.

"Helped?" A light, incredulous laugh trailed into my ear. "I wasn't aware you'd accomplished much so far. It's more likely he's involved in the whole plot."

My own suspicions were unacceptable when they came from Ronald. "Don't be silly. He's never even met Victor."

"Well, I don't like it. I think you should go and stay with Mom for a few days, just till Victor comes back. We don't know who the guy is. You may be the next one to disappear," he cautioned. The concern sounded genuine, and the idea that I might suddenly vanish from the face of Toronto wasn't exactly comforting either.

But still I'd rather live in fear than be locked up behind the stone walls and iron palings of the Strathroy mansion with those two pretentious stone lions snarling at passersby.

"I couldn't possibly. I have to be here, but thanks for the offer."

"I'll drop in after work. We'll go to the club for dinner. I promise to have you home early."

I agreed for two reasons. I didn't intend to see Sean and didn't much want to be alone, but more importantly, if Victor ended up in a jam because of this stolen violin business, you couldn't have better friends than the Strathroys. Any judge they weren't actually related to was bound to be a good friend.

"All right, I'll see you around five-thirty."

"Take good care of yourself now. I'll see you later."

It was a quarter to twelve, and I decided to give the apartment a lick and a promise because I was too jittery to sit still. I made a couple of phone calls; to Rhoda putting her off untill further notice, and to Marjie Klein, my best friend at work. All Marjie wanted to talk about was Victor's disappearance. I went over the highlights, she commiserated and assured me that nobody could be crazy enough to hurt that doll of a Victor. Of course they couldn't, I agreed, but when I hung up, I was very worried that they had. I felt a deep, heavy aching in my chest and a panicky desperation to find him.

CHAPTER 12

Ronald's call increased my doubts about Sean. It was true he'd only befriended me after he knew I was connected with Victor. A little more thinking convinced me he couldn't be Etherington, though. Victor had looked right at him and smiled at Casa Loma, so he hadn't recognized him. But Sean was more than a tourist; he knew too much, knew exactly what had happened. He'd led the conversation around to make it seem like logic, or inspiration, but in fact he knew. He couldn't know if he weren't a part of it all. Even the police didn't know, so he had to be on the other side of it. And therefore he knew where Victor was. I wouldn't let Sean back into the apartment, not when I was alone anyway, but I couldn't afford to lose track of him, either.

I thought of calling the police, but my ramblings would hardly be considered evidence. It would just take Sean out of commission for a few hours, and alert him that I was on to him. It would be better to follow Sean at a safe distance myself, and to do that, I had to keep in contact with him. That wouldn't be much trouble when he was at such pains to keep in contact with me. Why?

The answer was right there, staring me in the face. He stayed with me because they hadn't got the Stradivarius back, and he hoped I would lead them to it. Nothing could be plainer. Keeping the Strad under wraps was important to them until they'd arranged their financial affairs and left. And I, gullible fool, had taken Sean trotting up to Victor's cottage at Caledon, down to Union Station and all over, sharing my clues with him. He knew from his colleagues that Victor had locked the case at Union Station, and he was hanging around to wait for the key to turn up since it wasn't on my uncle, and he hadn't broken down and told them where it was. Sean must have been one disappointed man when the case held my old Adidas! That brought a travesty of a smile to my face.

Sean said he'd call me at noon; it was already five past twelve, and I didn't know what I'd say when he called. When the phone rang, I took three deep breaths to lower my nervous voice and said, "Hello."

"Hi. I've got to talk to you right away," Sean said excitedly.

Even that struck me as suspicious. It was a sure way to get me to see him, but I wouldn't let him come up here. "It's noon—why don't we meet somewhere for lunch? Where are you?"

"I'm at my hotel. I'll pick you up."

"I have to go downtown anyway. I'll meet you at the coffee shop at your hotel—the Delta Inn, isn't it?"

"Yeah, but . . ."

I cut in before he could object. "I'll be there in twenty minutes. Order me a cold salad plate, okay?"

"What, are you back on that vegetarian kick? I recommend the barbeque chicken."

Still playing the hick role to the hilt. "I'll just have a wing of yours."

"You're welcome to grab my wing any time you like. See you." He sounded exactly as usual.

Rather than waiting around for buses and subway trains, I took a taxi to his hotel. The busy hum of the city at noon hour, the accelerated rhythm of pedestrians and cars was still exciting to me. I'd lost the claustrophobic feeling of being in a glass-lined tunnel, and come to like the hectic, pellmell dash to catch lights, the zig to avoid the wave of oncoming walkers, the sudden feeling of déjà vu when I caught that doppel-ganger reflected life-size in a plate glass window pretending she was me.

Sean had cornered a table for us in the full coffee shop. He was sipping coffee and stood up and waved to catch my attention. An involuntary smile lit my face, then froze there as I remembered to distrust his friendly, open smile. The brown puppy eyes were suspect, the overlapped teeth not boyish but deceptive—in a word, crooked.

"That didn't take you long," he said when I slid into the seat.

"I splurged and took a taxi. What's the big news?"

"It's about the Strathroys. Of course, you already know I followed Eleanor. Her 'appointment' was at about a dozen exclusive shops at that little Rodeo Drive North mall near your place."

"I figured that was why you offered her a lift," I said noncommittally.

"It was worth a shot, but I don't see why you bothered to follow me?"

He made it a question, but didn't seem to notice when I evaded answering. "Ah heck, you spotted me."

"You weren't trying to hide from *me*, were you?" he laughed. "I was going to wait for you to catch up to me, but I figured we'd be less conspicuous alone. Those zebra stripes are designed for jungle camouflage, not the city," he added, looking at my dress. "Nice, but noticeable."

"I was just curious to see what she was up to," I said since he'd made that assumption. "But since you had her covered, I dropped out at Ronald's office."

A cheery, impatient smile gave advance notice that he had more revelations to come. "That's just where things got interesting."

"What happened?" My heart pounded in response to his excitement.

"She only stayed for about five minutes. I imagine it was Ronald she was seeing. I couldn't decide whether to go on following her or hang around and see what I could learn about Ronald. I was a bit bored with the window shopping, and if they're behind this scam, Ronald's a more likely agent than the old lady. I mean a fine gentleman like Ronald," he said with a grossly ironic look, "wouldn't let his Momma deal with creeps like Etherington. Besides, she's the one who let out about their knowing that Contessa in Italy."

I looked to see if he was joking. When I decided he wasn't,

I closed my mouth, then opened it again and laughed in disbelief. "Oh boy, are you off base! The Strathroys are loaded. A couple of hundred thousand wouldn't mean a thing to them. Their house alone would be worth a couple of million."

He shrugged. "Houses have been known to carry mortgages. And you don't know what I learned at Graymar Trust yet." His brows lifted in a significant way. "I hung around the switchboard for a minute. I heard a Mr. Stone leaving, telling the receptionist he'd be back at two. I chatted up the girl, a cute little blonde with green eyes," he added, with an infuriating smile. "I told her I had an appointment with Mr. Stone, but I couldn't remember the exact time. She asked me what it was about, said maybe one of the other men could help me out."

I gave a weary sigh. "Does all this eventually have something to do with Victor?"

"It has to do with Sir Ronald. I talked to the blonde between calls. There were a lot of calls for Ronald. Yesiree, I wouldn't be surprised if your Ronald is in the ejection seat. His boss—you *did* know he's only a junior partner there?—told him to get his tail into his office. I'd become a rich Texan looking for a safe place to hide a million or so bucks by that time. I offered to get Barbie a coffee to while away her hours at the board. Funny thing is, she knew damned well Stone wouldn't be back till two, but she didn't say so."

"You wouldn't think they'd hire an amnesiac to run a busy switchboard."

"It was the million bucks that made her forget," he admitted. "That's why I mentioned it. She said she had a coffee break coming up in ten minutes, and why didn't I wait and we'd go to the coffee shop together. So I waited and hinted around until I got her talking about Ronald."

"She must be a clever one not to have suspected anything." The food came and we began eating.

"She's not stupid, just indiscreet. I said if Stone wasn't in, maybe this Ronald Strathroy guy could handle my account. His name's on the door, you know, and she'd been talking to him on the phone as well. She got a kind of funny look on her face. 'Maybe Mr. Denver would be better,' she said. We waltzed that around for a while. Mr. Strathroy was a little young for such a large account, she thought. I told her I liked young men, they were more daring in their investments. A little too daring sometimes, she thought."

"What did you actually learn, other than Barbie's suspicions?"

"He was out of the office on Wednesday all right—Barbie didn't seem to know anything about Montreal."

"It's a secret. They were wise to keep it from loose-lips Barbie."

"I didn't actually learn for sure that Ronald's a crook, but the way she was talking, he's one hell of a poor account executive. I think he's been siphoning a little something from his clients, and has gotten caught at it. That's what *I* think," he announced triumphantly.

"That's ridiculous! They sent him to Montreal just this week to handle a big merger. They wouldn't do that if he were either a crook or stupid."

"That's where he was supposed to be the night of Victor's concert?"

"That's where he *was*."

"I thought I saw something on TV about it being a holiday in Quebec that day. The reason I noticed, I'd been thinking of hopping down to Montreal—till I met you."

No meltdown occurred this time. "He chose the holiday on purpose," I said, and explained the political situation. "And that was your great news, that one of the richest men in Toronto is a crook?"

"You must admit it's a strange coincidence, the Strathroys knowing that Italian Contessa who owned the stolen violin and being chummy with Victor. It's a link, is all I'm saying. They were at the villa—the scene of the first crime—and if Ronald had any funny ideas, he could have taken a look at the safety precautions the Contessa had installed."

"You don't have to draw me a picture, Sean. I understand what you're getting at, but as far as I'm concerned, it disproves that they had anything to do with it. They wouldn't point the finger at themselves. They'd make sure Etherington sold the violin in some other city or country. They wouldn't peddle it in their own backyard. Besides, they were in Quebec skiing at New Year's when the Strad was lifted."

"It was only around New Year's the thing was stolen, according to Bitwell. You never know. Victor was a perfect mark, being highly interested in a Stradivarius violin, having the dough, or being able to raise it. Eleanor knew he hadn't seen the thing, too, so he wouldn't recognize it. And since they were using another party—Etherington—to make the trade, they'd want to have it done here in Toronto where they could keep an eye on him. I'm not saying they're hardened criminals. They got caught in a tight corner, and pulled this one amateurish job. The very way it's been bungled points to amateurs."

"You heard Eleanor say she hadn't been to Italy for a few years. How did she manage to pluck the violin out of the Contessa's villa from across the ocean?"

"That's where Etherington comes in. Ronald told him the setup at the villa, and Etherington lifted the thing, brought it here, and arranged the sale."

"Lots of people would like to own a Stradivarius. They wouldn't pick a friend to play a dirty trick like that on," I said angrily. "You just don't understand, Sean. The Strathroys are . . ."

"I know, rich. Rich people have high expenses. It costs a lot to run a mansion, throw big parties. Do you know what Eleanor paid for a pair of shoes today?"

"Don't tell me you went into a ladies' shoe store and flirted with the clerk!"

"No, I'm going by the window. There wasn't a pair in there that cost less than two hundred bucks. Two hundred bucks— some of them were twice that. And she bought a pair."

"She'd hardly do that if they were stoney broke, would she?"

"Maybe she doesn't know how Ronald has screwed things up," was his solution to that problem.

"Ronald does not screw things up. You're just jealous. Admit it, you hate his guts."

"Hate them? I never even knew he had any. How can you fall for a Mommie's boy like Ronald? According to Barbie, all he thinks about is his haircut and clothes."

"That's an accusation Barbie will never have to make against you. Ronald's a lot of fun on a date."

"Yeah, more fun than a barrel of Woody Allens. *Now* we're having a fight, right?"

"A discussion. Shall we discuss something more useful than Barbie and Ken? *Ronald*!" I corrected hastily.

A slow, lazy smile crept across his face, baring his crooked teeth. "Her brain might have been by Mattel, but the body was by Fisher."

"Fisher-Price, you mean?"

He ignored it. "Do you know, we forgot to ask Bitwell if Victor described this Etherington guy to him. Why don't you give him a call now?" he suggested.

"I already did. He just said he was an Englishman, old-school-tie type."

"That's all?"

Since Sean already knew about Etherington, there was no point concealing the rest of it, and I told him.

"Not much help. Anyone can put on a Brit accent—or a moustache and glasses for that matter," he said pensively.

We talked about the case all through lunch, but Sean was too wily to reveal anything. I was becoming terribly, terribly impatient. Somewhere Victor was locked up—if we were lucky. I willed down the image that reared its ugly head of my uncle's inert body dumped into a box in some dark alley. When the waitress brought the check, Sean put the bill on his hotel tab. He was still in room 327.

"Is there anything special you want to do this afternoon?" he asked.

I said no, because what I meant to do necessitated getting away from him first.

"There's the business of Victor's own Guarneri violin. We never did find that."

"I just want to be alone. I need to think."

His fingers closed over mine and he squeezed them consolingly. "Try not to worry too much, Cassie." His fingers were warm, his smile loving. "Something will break soon. You'll see. Why, I wouldn't be surprised if your uncle got away from them and came back, playing his Stradivarius."

Tears smarted in my eyes, but I blinked them away. "Sure." I felt betrayed by his sympathy that looked so genuine, so caring.

"I'll take you home now," he said and got up.

"I'll take the subway. It'll be a distraction for me. Thanks for lunch, Sean."

"See you tonight?"

"I still owe you dinner, but I'm seeing an old friend tonight."

"Ronald?"

"If you want to know, you'll have to hire a detective."

"I think I know already. See if you can find out anything from him."

We held hands as we went into the lobby and toward the front door. "Will you be late?" was his next uncertain question. I knew what he was working up to. Could he come over after?

"No way. I mean to be in bed before ten. I'm bushed."

"I'll call you tomorrow then. Take care."

"You too. Bye."

I blew him a kiss and had to leave the hotel as he stood right at the door. After half a block, I bought a newspaper and went back to the lobby to spy, like a second rate private eye in a thirties movie with my face hidden behind the paper. I angled myself for a view of the door and waited. In a quarter of an hour, I spotted Sean's blue checked shirt and western hat leaving. A cab pulled up and he got in. Any trip far enough away to require a cab left me time to search his room.

It's dangerous the way a room clerk will hand over a key to any respectable-looking person who comes to the desk and asks for it nonchalantly, using the patron's name and room number. The key to room 327 was handed over without so much as a question or raised eyebrow. My insides were quaking as I rode up in the elevator but tightened to a painful knot when I inserted the key in the lock.

It was a perfectly ordinary sort of middle-class hotel room: beige walls, flowered spread and drapes, cheap reproductions on the wall, minimal furnishings. A tan nylon bag with imitation leather bindings sat on the luggage bench at the end of the bed. Sean had unpacked his jackets and trousers, but there were shirts and undies still in the bag. A wad of laundry was tossed into the plastic bag provided. I didn't bother with it.

There was absolutely nothing interesting in the pockets of the jackets and trousers hanging in the closet. Both the jackets

and the Fruit of the Loom underwear in the case looked brand
new, but the jeans and shirts were well worn. There were no
personal papers anywhere, no pictures, just the local newspapers open at the stories about Victor, but that was hardly
unusual. A person doesn't really bring much but clothes and
toilet articles to a hotel room.

His Old Spice toiletries and a Bic razor were on the counter
in the bathroom along with Crest toothpaste, Butler dental
floss, a new red toothbrush and a black comb. All small,
travelling-size things, probably picked up here. He was the
messy kind of bather who used all the towels when he
showered and shaved and threw them in the tub after.

There didn't seem to be anything unusual or suspicious in
the room. I had hoped for a passport at least, preferably bearing
some name other than Sean Bradley. Just before leaving, I took
one last look in the tan case. There was a bag of toffee candies
there. I pulled them out, and saw they were made in England.
Of course, candy made in England was available in Toronto. I
examined a couple of white shirts folded in the bottom; they
had English labels, too, and they weren't new. A hardware
merchant from North Platte didn't wear imported, expensive
shirts, but I bet Etherington and his pals did. The hairs on my
arms lifted. I stood perfectly still, temporarily shocked into
paralysis. It was true then; open, friendly Sean was my enemy.

I noticed a side pocket on the luggage, on the outside, for
convenience. There was a bulge in it, and my knees were
shaking so hard I had to sit on the edge of the bed as I unzipped
it. The first item my searching fingers encountered was a small
piece of metal, which turned out to be an expensive Girard-
Perregaux watch, not new. Had Sean nicked it, or had he
bought the cheap Timex to reinforce his hick image?

Already my fingers were rifling below the watch for the stiff
manila envelope below. I opened it carefully. It contained
nothing but a few photographs. He had taken pictures of Victor
and some other man, not together, but in the same place. The
other man had a moustache and wore tinted shades. He wore a
blazor and what could very well be an old school tie. I'd never
seen the man before in my life.

There was one of this man, Etherington I assumed, entering
a restaurant called simply the Trattoria. I didn't recognize it,

but it was somewhere downtown, and the phone book could tell me where. The pictures had been taken from across the street, and the end of a passing street car identified the city as Toronto. Etherington was carrying a paper bag large enough to hold a violin. There was also one of Victor entering the Trattoria, with his violin case under his arm. The next one was of Victor coming out, wearing a big smile, still with the violin case, which would contain the Stradivarius now. Etherington was in the next shot. He wore the same expression as my uncle.

There were other pedestrians on the street as well—it was in a busy part of town. So it was at the Trattoria that Victor had bought the Stradivarius from Etherington, and Sean had known it all along. He had visual proof, so he not only knew it, he had been there and taken pictures. The old familiar "why" was back to bedevil me. He'd gone to make sure Etherington followed instructions, but why take pictures? To have something to blackmail Etherington with if he turned unreliable?

Sean wasn't a policeman or he would have made his arrest then and there. No, he definitely wasn't on the right side of the law. Of course, I had suspected it before, but it was desolating to have the proof. Desolating, and dangerous, and frightening. My heart beat like a jackhammer as I stuffed the pictures into my purse, the manila envelope back into the side pocket, zipped the pocket, and left the room as though the hounds of hell were after me.

In the lobby, I threw the key on the desk, caught a taxi and went straight back to the apartment. I chained the door and examined the pictures again. There hadn't been any camera in Sean's room, but I had some unclear memory of seeing one in his rented car. The pictures, four in all, were as I remembered, but now I looked more closely at the other pedestrians in the street.

A few steps behind Victor as he entered the restaurant was a figure that looked familiar. I checked the picture of Victor coming out, and by that time the short man in the dark suit had turned to face the camera, using the pretext of lighting a cigarette to hang around. He was the swarthy little man who had been at the Casa Loma with Sean and had gotten out of the elevator this morning to call on Betty Friske. I now had three suspects to hand over to the police and the address of two of them. I reached for the phone to call them before Sean had time to check out of the hotel. That would be his first move when he discovered the pictures were missing.

Lieutenant Marven wasn't in but was expected soon. I left my name and asked him to come to my apartment the second he arrived. It seemed better to deal with the man in charge of the case. After this, there was nothing to do but sit and wait, and think, and repine a little. I jumped into the air when the phone rang, but it was only another party interested in buying the cottage.

As I remembered the swarthy little man visiting next door yesterday, I began to feel unsafe there alone and decided to call Ronald, hoping he could get away early and keep me company.

"Ron, it's me, Cassie. I'd like to talk to you—about Sean. I had lunch with him, and he's—involved in this business, as you thought," I said warily.

"Involved? What do you mean?" he asked sharply. "Did he try to hurt you?"

"No, he doesn't even know I know. I've called the police. Marven will be coming over as soon as he gets in. I was kind of hoping you could be here when he comes."

"But what's happened? How did you find out about Sean?" he persisted, and I told him about the pictures.

"Good Lord, you could be in danger if he finds out. I'll be right over."

"How soon?"

"I just left," he said and hung up.

It was reassuring to know a friend was on his way, full of concern. The future looked brighter now. The police would pick up Sean and force him to reveal where Victor was locked up. He had to be locked up and not dead. My uncle would be freed and we'd find out where he'd hidden the Stradivarius. All I had to do was wait. And wait, and wait. Ten minutes, fifteen—what was keeping them?

My mind roamed over the case, concentrating on Sean Bradley. How well he'd played his role of small-town rube. He'd cooked for me, offered to vacuum—why couldn't men really be like that? I couldn't picture Ronald cooking, but then Ronald's wife would have maids. And Ronald had sounded extremely eager to run to my aid.

I looked at the pictures again. Victor had left the apartment with his violin case, but Etherington wasn't carrying the Guarneri when he left the restaurant, so obviously Victor hadn't taken it with him. He must have left it here, in this apartment, but where? Even before the break-in, it wasn't here. The apartment was so small there wasn't even room for all the stuff I'd brought from McGill with me. I had a couple of boxes of books and things locked in his locker in the basement.

The thought no sooner floated across my mind than I realized Victor might have locked his del Gesù there for safekeeping. In his excitement, he might have forgotten to take it out of the case when he left, and decided to store it in the locker rather than come back upstairs. It wouldn't take him more than a few steps out of his way since the lockers were in a corridor just a step from the parking garage. I'd go down and look as soon as Marven or Ronald arrived. What was keeping them? Seventeen minutes now since I'd phoned.

I couldn't wait any longer. I had to know, and besides, I'd probably meet Marven or Ronald on his way in from the garage. The lockers were safer than this apartment as far as that went. Betty Friske might have a key to the front door for all I knew. Somebody had entered with a key and taken Victor's cigars. The apartment suddenly seemed less safe than the rest of the building. I got the locker key from the kitchen, picked up my apartment keys and ran for the elevator.

CHAPTER 13

There were no elegant mirrors or carpets in the passage to the storage lockers. Plain painted walls and a gray concrete floor were good enough for this out-of-the-way corner, but it was well lit. I'd only been to the locker room once before and couldn't remember whether the lights were turned off that time, as they were now. I stood irresolutely at the door, then reached in my hand and felt for the light switch.

There was just the rough concrete wall, and I looked around to see if the switch was outside. There was one there, but it didn't turn on the lights inside. It didn't seem to do anything. Afraid I'd started some air conditioner or auxiliary engine, I flicked it off again and took a step into the room. Damned switch—where was it? And I didn't have a flashlight or even a match or lighter.

If Victor's locker had been at the far end of the room, I wouldn't have gone in, but it was just the third from the door, dimly visible in the light from the hallway. Three steps and I'd know; it would be too cowardly to turn back now. I strode boldly forward, got the key into the padlock and unhooked it. And there it was, Victor's del Gesù, its expensive curves resting daintily on top of my boxes of books. He must have been in a hurry because he hadn't bothered to cover it.

He treated that violin like the heir to a fabled throne. Success drove out the last residue of fear. I picked up the violin and saw the bow wedged in behind it. I snatched it up, juggling till I had the violin and bow in one hand, the key and padlock in the other and juggled some more untill I got the lock back through the hole to resecure the locker.

Afterwards, when I regained consciousness, I wasn't sure whether there had actually been a faint, shuffling sound behind me, or I'd dreamed it. In any case, I didn't see whomever stunned me from behind. There was no stray whiff of Old Spice or anything else to help identify my assailant. Just that stunning blow on the side of my head, followed by a shower of light and then by strange, wheeling balls of yellow sun on a purpley-blue-black background.

It would have taken a man to carry me from the locker room to the car that transported me to where I now rested. A woman, (Betty Friske?), couldn't have done it alone. I lay spread on the floor of a huge room. The silent furnace towering above me wasn't the size of a house furnace. I staggered to my feet while the balls of light shrank smaller and smaller till they were only pinpricks, each sending a needle of pain through my temples. I shook them away and groped my way up from the floor, holding against the cold steel of the furnace for balance. My watch must have stopped. It had to be more than ten minutes since I left the apartment. Ten minutes wasn't long enough to have carried me off to the hiding place.

It was the blow that made me so stupid. Of course, I was still in the apartment building! Whoever hit me had only dragged or carried me down the hall and shoved me into the furnace room. My dress didn't show signs of dragging which confirmed that my attacker was a man. Both the violin and the locker key were gone. The key was probably still in the locker room, but I had no intention of going alone to look for it.

I crept timidly to the door, looked up and down the empty corridor, then ran like a hare to the staircase and up to the building superintendant's apartment. You'd think a building superintendant would always be there, on hand for emergencies, but he didn't answer the door. The fear was receding, and a hot anger was following in its wake. My knees were quite steady as I ran up the next stairway to the lobby. Lieutenant Marven was just coming out of the parking elevator.

"Miss Newton!" he exclaimed, and stared at me as though I were a ghost. I was probably the color of one. My arms and legs were dusty from rolling on the floor, and there was a bump rising on the side of my head, but that wouldn't show.

"Come with me!" I said, and pulled him through the door, back down the stairs to the locker room. "He might still be there."

"Who? What's happened?"

I was hoping when Marven reached into his pocket that he'd draw a gun; he pulled out a flashlight about as big as a pencil. "In there," I whispered as we approached the locker room door. I gave him the gist of my story in low whispers. He carefully opened the door. The light was on to make a liar of me. I flicked the switch outside the door, and it went off.

"It wasn't working before!" I assured him.

Victor's locker door was closed; the key was in the padlock, and when Marven opened the door, the del Gesù was back on its perch atop my books. He lunged forward. "Is this the Stradivarius Dr. Bitwell told us about?"

When I told him what it was, his interest in the violin lessened considerably, but he took it and the bow out of the locker and examined them. "We'll go up to the apartment and discuss this," he said, tucking them under his arm. His manner had chilled noticeably. He thought I had staged the whole thing for what purpose I couldn't even imagine.

Ronald was outside my door when we reached the seventeenth floor and showed a gratifying concern for my filthy condition and bumped head. He poured me a drink of scotch and soda while I outlined my day's activities to Marven.

"At least your assailant didn't get the pictures," Marven said. His spirits improved to learn there was a bit of tangible evidence. "Let's have a look at them."

But when I rifled in my purse, I came up empty-handed. Incredibly, the pictures were gone. I felt guilty, like the culprit instead of the victim. We looked all around the sofa, the coffee table, and later in desperation he had me go through the kitchen and my bedroom, though I knew perfectly well they weren't there. At last, I had to admit they were gone. Marven's cold gray eyes turned on me in irony, too disdainful to be quite accusing.

"Correct me if I'm wrong, Miss Newton, but are you telling me that you were hit on the head by an unknown assailant in a dark room, whose light worked perfectly when I tried it a few minutes later? This violent assailant then proceeded to remove you to the furnace room and didn't bother taking the violin you had found?"

"He took the pictures!" I pointed out. "They're gone!"

"I see. This remarkably clairvoyant assailant knew you had pictures in your apartment that would incriminate him? He's a magician as well, is he, that he had time to come up seventeen floors and get into a locked apartment after bundling you off to the furnace room? Or did you leave the door open for him?"

"No, obviously he has a key."

"Who has a key, other than yourself and Mr. Mazzini?"

"Whoever kidnapped my uncle. Sean Bradley, if you want a name. I told you, I found the pictures in his hotel room. He's the one who doesn't want you to see them."

"What exactly is the relationship between yourself and Mr. Bradley?" Marven asked. Ronald listened sharply but didn't butt in.

"Acquaintances. I've been seeing him as I think he is involved in my uncle's disappearance."

"Why didn't you tell the police about this?"

"I just became suspicious today."

The story was so confusing that I began at the beginning and tried to make some sense of it. I told him about my first meeting with Sean at the Casa Loma and our whole past history about the little dark man, and his being in the pictures, and having visited Betty Friske. Since I had been derelict in keeping certain matters from the police, I omitted the first apartment break-in and Victor's stolen cigars. Another mystery within a mystery. But I explained about Sean's interest in the Stradivarius, his knowing about it before he reasonably could have known if he were innocent.

"What's the problem, Lieutenant?" Ronald asked stiffly. "Miss Newton has solved your case for you. Why don't you get down to the Delta Inn and arrest Mr. Bradley before he gets away? He won't stick around long once he realizes the pictures are missing. They absolutely incriminate him."

"It seemed wiser to allow Miss Newton a few minutes to collect her thoughts after her accident. Odd Mr. Bradley would hold onto the pictures if they were as damning as you think. Criminals usually dispose of evidence, Mr. Strathroy."

"He was keeping them to blackmail Mr. Etherington," I explained.

"The only place Etherington exists, so far as I know, is in pictures which I have not seen. As to those pictures——there are safer places to keep incriminating evidence than in one's own hotel room as you tell me Mr. Bradley did."

"He had no reason to think he was suspected," Ronald said.

"Why would a criminal lead his victim so close to the truth as you say Bradley did?" Marven asked. "According to your story, it was Bradley who came up with the idea of the stolen Stradivarius."

"Yes, because he hoped I could lead him to it," I explained.

He turned a pair of brightly suspicious eyes on me and asked softly, "And did you?"

"Now see here, Lieutenant," Ronald blustered. "Are you accusing Miss Newton of being involved in this? I want you to know she is a very good friend of my family. I'll call my lawyer, Cassie," he added aside to me. "if Mr. Bradley escapes due to your negligence, Marven, you can expect to account to the Attorney General for it."

If Marven was disturbed by this threat, he did an excellent job of concealing it. "The innocent have no reason to be so jumpy, Mr. Strathroy. I didn't bring along my handcuffs, nor am I accusing Miss Newton of anything. In our position, we have to consider all possibilities. The fact of the matter is, Mr. Mazzini bought stolen merchandise and was soon made aware of that fact——if he didn't know it already——but chose not to inform the police. There are two theories as to why he disappeared. One of them involves his desire to keep the violin . . ."

It took a few minutes to make sense of this. "Are you saying he rigged the whole thing——he did it to make you think someone had stolen the violin from him so he wouldn't have to give it back? That's crazy!" I scoffed.

"He could have claimed the violin was stolen without disappearing," Ronald added.

"He could have, but then if he'd reported it at once, we'd have caught the fellows and saved ourselves a great deal of bother. We now have the RCMP pestering us as well. There was more than a Stradivarius violin stolen from the Carpani villa—a great deal more. A fortune in jewelry that someone is trying to sell underground. We've only now got a description of it from the Mounties since Dr. Bitwell decided we *might* be interested to know about the stolen violin."

When we didn't reply to this, Marven continued, "They might have sold half the stuff by now for all we know. As for Mr. Mazzini's peculiar disappearance, we're meant to think his kidnappers have the Stradivarius, and they've had time to get clean away so we won't pester Mr. Mazzini unduly about it."

"My uncle is not a crook!" I shouted, feeling akin to Richard Nixon. "And they haven't gotten clean away. One of them is at the Delta Inn," I reminded him.

"I'll see what Bradley has to say." Marven's cold, suspicious eye's flickered over me as he went to pick up the phone. In a bored voice, he sent two policemen to the Delta Inn and said he'd meet them there later. Then he left.

"I don't believe this!" I said to Ronald. "He thinks Victor took the violin and ran. That's what he thinks. He sure doesn't know much about my uncle if he thinks he'd spend a fortune on a violin he can't play in public."

"The man's an idiot. I'm going to phone the Attorney General's office and lodge a complaint. But first, Cassie, I wish you'd tell me exactly what's been going on between you and this Bradley guy. How did he know about the Carpani Strad before Bitwell told him?"

"He didn't know it was the Carpani Strad then or didn't admit it anyway. Bitwell's the one who identified it. He just talked his way around till it seemed logical to assume a Stradivarius violin was involved. He did it all so I'd lead him to it. He picked my brains clean, Ron."

While we had a Scotch, I told him about someone's having been in the apartment the night Victor disappeared, looking for the violin. I told him about the locker key from Union Station and how we found my Adidas in Victor's violin case when we opened the locker. I told him everything I could think of because I felt so guilty and needed to confess to someone.

Ronald listened quietly, assuring me that I hadn't been an

idiot but just a little too trusting. "That's not a bad fault in a lady," he said warmly when I had finished. "And Bradley thought the violin must be hidden at Casa Loma?"

"Yes, we went there and looked all over, but it wasn't there."

"It would take days to look all over," he pointed out.

"All over the places Victor had been. He wasn't there long, you know. I figured the locker area and the music room were about all he had time for, and we looked there. Unless he met someone outside the place and handed it over to him for safekeeping, I just don't know where it could be. It vanished. Whoever kidnapped Victor didn't get it because my uncle had obviously disposed of it before he got to Union Station and hid the case in that locker. He carried the empty case to fool them. Crazy, huh?"

"Weird." Ron sat puzzling for a while longer. "Hey, we were supposed to be going out for dinner tonight. Are you up to it?"

"My head aches like the devil."

"You don't look so hot. You're pale as a ghost. Do you want me to call a doctor, have him take a look at that bump?"

"I'm all right."

"Why don't you take a sleeping pill and go to bed? I'll call you later."

"Do you have to go?"

But of course Ronald was hungry even if I wasn't. And I couldn't conjure up an image of Ronald in a kitchen. The Scotch was making me pleasantly sleepy; I didn't need a pill and didn't have one in the house for that matter. I'd rest for a few hours, then maybe when Ron called, he'd take me out for a late night snack.

"I want to make a few calls," he said. "I don't care for the way Marven's handling this case. I'm going to speak to the super on the way out, too, and get your lock changed. Okay?"

My heart congealed. I was in enough danger that I had to start taking precautions for my safety, maybe my life. In my worst imaginings, it had never come to this. "Good idea. Meanwhile I'll put on the chain and wedge a table or something in front of the door."

"Call me as soon as you wake up. Promise?"

At the door he pulled my head against his shoulder and ran his fingers over my bump, while his lips pressed my forehead. "You should put an ice pack on that, darling," he murmured. Ronald never called me "darling" before. His voice sounded sexy with his lips nibbling my ear. He put one finger under my chin and tilted my face up to his.

There in the shadowed hall, he looked very handsome in a refined, dignified way. Not macho and rugged like Sean but very sexy. What an idiot I'd been, virtually ignoring Ron. He had everything: looks, family, money, and now he was being kind. And in a pinch, he was the one who had the clout to extricate Victor if by any chance Marven was right. That, unfortunately, was a possibility, however remote, and however strongly I denied it in public.

His lips brushed mine gently, very gently. I put my arms around his neck and coerced him into a better kiss. He even offered to stay, but my head was aching badly, and I don't think he meant to stay anywhere but in bed with me, so I let him go. I went to bed alone as soon as I'd put the chain on and dragged an armchair in front of the door. Now anger mingled with my fear—anger that I should be in this position when I hadn't done anything wrong.

CHAPTER 14

Of course, as soon as I got between the covers, I was wide awake. My mind was not only active, but hyperactive. I went over all the happenings of the past few days, one step at a time. About an hour later, I had come to two conclusions. The first was that Marven was wrong to think Victor had run off so he could keep the violin. Not if he couldn't broadcast it to the world—no way. The second was that the darned thing was still at the Casa Loma. It had to be.

When you eliminate the impossible, then what's left is true, however improbable, as Sean had said. Victor had bought the Strad, he'd taken it to Bitwell and learned it was stolen. Whatever his ultimate plan, he didn't want to phone the police immediately. I thought he hoped to sweet talk it out of the contessa. A Stradivarius would get him good coverage for his European tour. He must have noticed someone was following him, and he hid the violin at Casa Loma and led his followers a merry chase, probably loving every minute of it. They'd managed to catch him, presumably in the parking garage right here at the apartment and were holding him captive. That much had to be true; there was no other logical explanation.

He must have the heart of a Samurai not to have revealed to them where he hid the violin. Oh, but he didn't have the body of one, poor little Victor! At least they couldn't be torturing him, or he would have told. Victor hates pain. He carries on like a baby when he gets a little burn or cuts himself shaving.

Maybe he figured his silence was all that was keeping him
alive. Once they got the violin, then they wouldn't need
him . . . and he could identify them afterwards.

The longer I thought, the wider awake I became. I had
already identified one of them, and if Sean learned that, how
long would I go on breathing? The phone suddenly rang,
upsetting my train of thought, but a call from Ron was
welcome, and I ran to answer it.

"Hi, Cassie. How are you?" Sean asked, as calmly as
though he didn't know I had a welt the size of a large walnut
on my head.

Speech failed me. I just looked in disbelief at the receiver,
and wished Sean were there, so I could throw it at him. While
my blood seethed, I began planning how to trap him. "Just
fine. Where are you?" This was very necessary to know, not
that I could count on him to tell the truth.

"Sure you're all right? You sound a little funny."

"I'm all right. Any special reason for calling?"

"Just checking out a few things. I took another tour of Casa
Loma. I'm on my way back to the hotel now. Can I come over
later—after your dinner date?"

He was pretending he hadn't been back to his room, didn't
know the pictures were gone, and therefore had no reason to
have koshed me. I played along with it for my own reasons. It
occurred to me that as he *did* know, I should perhaps intimate
something of the attack, but not, of course, hint that I thought
he was involved.

"I decided to cancel on Ron. I was hoping you'd call.
Actually a little something did come up. I'll tell you about it
when you get here. I've got the steaks marinating. Let's dress
up and make a gala affair of it. I don't suppose you have an
evening suit in your room?" I had to get him back to the hotel
where the police were waiting for him.

"No, but I have a clean shirt and tie."

"It'll have to do. How long will it take you to shower and
change?"

"Ten minutes. I'll be there within half an hour. You can
open the wine to breathe. Or am I bringing the wine?"

"It's already breathing away. Hurry up now."

"I will. And Cassie . . ." The pause that followed could

best be described as about nine months pregnant. I held my breath and listened.

"What is it?"

"Are you alone?"

The question sent a cold scalpel of fear through my vitals. "Yes."

"I hope you've got the lock on that door?"

"I have. Why, are you worried about me?" My attempt at lightness fell resoundingly flat.

"Yeah, kind of. Because of your breaker-in having Victor's key. We should get that lock changed."

"That's a good idea, but meanwhile the chain is on." And I thought I'd put another chair in front of the door, too, as soon as he hung up. Ron had spoken to the super, and presumably the lock would be changed in the morning.

"Keep it on till I get there. I've had another unsettling idea. Do you want it now, or later?"

There wouldn't be any "later." "Let's hear it."

"I don't want to scare the bejeebbers out of you, but I've been thinking. They haven't managed to break Victor down, to get him to tell them where the violin is."

"I know. I thought of that."

"Yeah, did you think of the only other lever they have? You. I'll be over in two shakes. Meanwhile, keep that door locked and bolted. Maybe I should bring my pyjamas. I don't like to think of you there alone. You and me together now—that'd be—uh—safer," he said, and gave a lecherous little laugh.

I felt about as safe as woman with a switchblade at her throat. "We'll see. You don't have to wear your jammies, do you?"

"As a matter of fact, I don't own a pair. I sleep in my BVDs." He even lied about brands. His Fruit of the Looms were what he slept in. "You can put the potatoes in the oven. I'll be there soon. I like mine rare—the steak, that is."

"Do you mean red, or pink?"

"Just so it's not brown all the way through. But as long as you're serving it, I'll even eat it burned." His voice had turned to marshmallow.

"This line is pretty well-done too. How do you like your potatoes?"

"You decide—I suggest you decide well-done, like my line." And intimate rumble of laughter lurked along the line.

"Got it."

I didn't even bother hanging up the receiver, but just pushed down the lever to get a dial tone, and phoned Marven.

"This is Miss Newton. What have you done about Bradley?"

"I have two men at the hotel; one in the lobby, one in his room. He hasn't showed up yet, but he hasn't checked out."

"He's on his way there—if he's telling the truth. I just had a call from him."

"What did he say?"

I told him, and he listened politely. But when I finished, he threw another scare into me. "There's no reason to believe what he said. Nothing else he told you checks out."

My body went into a state of shock. "What do you mean? What have you found out?"

"We've been doing a little checking. There's no Sean Bradley in North Platte. There's a John Bradford, but he's not a hardware store owner. And there's a Sean . . ."

"I get the idea. What do you think he's up to? Do you think he'll really come? Because if he does, I want some protection."

"I'll have a plainclothesman in the lobby."

"I want him here, in my apartment. And hurry for God's sake! He could have been phoning from across the street for all we know."

"I'll take care of it. I'll be in touch," he said, and hung up.

The next ten minutes stand out in my short life as ten of the most anxious, right up there with waiting for the root canal work to begin. I actually felt nauseous from fear. When life returned to my rigid limbs, I armed myself with a hammer, put that second chair in front of the door, and a table in front of that for good measure. That done, I climbed on the chair closest to the door and stared out the peephole. The hall was empty. I put my ear to the door, listening for signs of a man who was quite possibly coming to murder me and another who was coming to prevent him. What was keeping the policeman? This was my ungainly position when the phone rang again.

I climbed down and picked up the receiver without saying hello. My nerves were performing strange tricks on my vocal chords. I tried to speak, but nothing came out. When Marven said hello, my heart slid back down my throat, and I managed to squeak out a greeting.

"We've got him," Marven said. "He arrived at the hotel shortly after you phoned. He was telling the truth about that at least."

My body collapsed in relief. Till then I hadn't realized it was as tight as a spring. "Did he tell you where Mr. Mazzini is?"

"He just returned to his hotel room. My men are bringing him in now. I haven't spoken to him yet. I just wanted to set your mind at rest."

"I want to hear the minute you learn anything."

"I'll let you know, Miss Newton. Do you still want that plainclothesman? I guess there's no point now. I can radio him back. We're a bit short-handed down here."

"You can have him unless Bradley escapes. Oh, by the way, does he have the Stradivarius violin? He said he'd been at the Casa Loma."

"No, he doesn't."

"Thank you, Lieutenant Marven."

"Thank you, Miss Newton," he said so pleasantly I had to wonder if he'd had a call from the Attorney General's office.

I hung up and smiled wanly at the phone. That just about evened the score with Mr. Sean Bradley or whoever he was.

I pushed the furniture back into place and sat down to resume normal breathing. My stomach was soon telling me by means of violent spasms that I had recovered. I called Ronald to let him know the news and to tell him he could come over. Eleanor answered.

"He asked me to call you around nine, Cassie," she said. "He completely forgot an appointment he had this evening. Some friends from Oxford are visiting, and he'd promised to show them around town, but he means to be home early. He planned to call you around ten."

"Please, ask him to call."

I outlined briefly the interesting things that had happened. Eleanor was amazed. I could hear voices in the background and knew she was entertaining, which was fine with me. I'd have the pleasure of giving Ron all the details first hand. Seeing Ron at ten was better than not seeing him at all but not as good as seeing him now. My stomach spasms were increasing so I went to the kitchen to forage.

In the fridge I saw the remains of the food Sean had brought. Canadian bacon and eggs, cream. "I switched us to half and half," he'd said, and I had found him so adorable. He had seemed genuinely frightened when he got the doorman to open the door. He'd even offered to vacuum. Damn! This was no time to be remembering all the sweet things he'd done. He'd only done them to con me into leading him to the violin. But he'd done them so naturally.

The same as he lied so naturally tonight on the phone, telling me to be careful in that concerned voice that sounded totally sincere. Telling me I might be in jeopardy from whomever was holding Victor. Why tell me that unless he was a sadist? And that hint to stay overnight—he'd have done it, too, if the plan had left time for it. And now he was being hauled down to the police station, probably in handcuffs.

My stomach spasms stopped. Suddenly, I couldn't even think of food, but coffee was a good idea. I boiled water, measured the coffee, thinking all the time about Sean. I didn't have to coerce him into a good kiss. He did that very naturally, too—to Betty Friske as well as me. And chatting up the cute blonde in Ron's office. I bet Ron never chatted her up.

Was I actually feeling jealous about that oversexed criminal? I hoped they used a blackjack on him. I phoned Marven again and asked if Mr. Bradley had arrived yet. "I only called you five minutes ago," he said rather curtly. The Strathroy influence didn't completely cover me yet.

"Remember to call me as soon as you learn anything."

"Why don't you go to bed, Miss Newton? It's not likely we'll get this tied up tonight. This isn't *Hill Street Blues*."

"More like the Keystone Kops!" I snipped and slammed down the receiver.

Idiot. I solved the case, and he couldn't even beat a confession out of Sean in one night. How long would it take him to bring Victor home? I called Marjie Klein to do some boasting and complaining, and learned she was at work.

"At this hour? What's going on?"

"There's a wedding at Casa Loma," her roomie told me.

"They wanted one of us to be there to steer the guests around, and Marjie volunteered. It's time and a half."

"Tell her Cassie called, will you?"

"Will do."

I poured the coffee and used some of Sean's half and half. The wedding parties at Casa Loma were held in the beautiful conservatory with the marble floor. They spilled over into Peacock Alley and the library, too—the main rooms downstairs were all open really, but the guides tried to keep the party more or less in the east wing of the floor. It was a gorgeous place for a wedding. I'd worked a few of them myself like Marjie was doing tonight.

Suddenly I knew I was going to work this one, too. Not officially, but it was a good time to search for the violin. It had to be there, somewhere in that ninety-eight room castle. Sean Bradley knew it—he'd gone back but he hadn't found it. I knew the place better. I knew every nook and cranny. And what better time to find it than now, tonight, while there was the safety of lots of lights and people without the nuisance of tours passing to interrupt me? I could wander among the guests at leisure secure in the knowledge that Sean Bradley was under lock and key.

I wouldn't wear my guide uniform but a fancy dress to blend in with the wedding party. Before you could say Antonio Stradivari I was wriggling into my expensive white wisp and calling a taxi.

CHAPTER 15

In Toronto, Casa Loma is familiarly known as the "House on the Hill." Of course, it's at the top of the hill twenty-four hours a day, but its preeminent position is more dramatically seen at night with the flood lights playing on turrets, battlements and chimneys. A splendid castle with lights glowing in dozens of windows was an unlikely spot to instill terror in a woman's heart, but something inside me shrank as the taxi approached it. I was beseiged by vague, free-floating anxieties.

There was nothing to be afraid of, I told myself. Sean was in custody. I assumed Etherington had been saddled with the job of guarding Victor since neither of them had been seen since the kidnapping. I'd just go in and make a leisurely tour of all the spots Victor could possibly have hidden the violin. There weren't that many when his brief visit was taken into consideration. Of the ninety-eight rooms, about ninety could be ignored. I wouldn't waste a minute thinking about the tunnel or stables, the towers, or even anything above the first floor.

I paid off the cab driver and went into the hallway. The hum of a crowd at play was reassuring. Lots of people—safety in numbers. The wedding dinner was over, and the dancing had begun. Hordes of people roamed through the halls, looking anachronistic in their modern garb, and a few were dancing in the Great Hall. The bride, in a long gown and Spanish-style headdress, was laminated against the groom's tuxedo, her eyes closed, her head resting on her new husband's shoulder as they swayed to the music.

142

I eased myself into a dark, inconspicous corner to take a long look around for a hiding place. There weren't that many spots given the size of the room. The long-case clock had a glass front so obviously he hadn't hidden the violin in there. The sofas and chairs weren't against the walls but were more or less free standing which made it unlikely he'd pushed his violin under one of them. It would be visible from a doorway. There were tables and plants but nowhere to hide a violin.

I came out and looked right at Peacock Alley which is just a long, fancy hall leading to the Conservatory. When I saw Victor leaving, he hadn't been coming from that direction. He had been coming from the direction of his favorite spot, the music room. The valuables there are roped off to prevent people from fooling around with the Steinway, the old harp and other things. Other than the instruments, there's not a lot to engage the tourists' interest, and in the middle of a wedding feast, the room was deserted, or so I thought until I stepped in.

There was one man there, leaning over the Steinway. He'd hopped the rope and was playing the piano with two fingers. The guide in me wanted to tell him to stop, but tonight I was pretending I was a guest.

He looked over his shoulder and said, "It's out of tune." I noticed he had a moustache and an English accent. I'm not personally familiar with the pattern of English school ties, but I imagined they were probably a lot like the finely-striped blue and red and gold one this man wore. There was a crest on his blazor. While I stared, speechless, he smiled and started playing chopsticks, all wrong. Was he the man from the picture? There was some similarity—the same general type . . .

I looked over my shoulder to make sure there were people in view close behind before speaking. "Do you sing, too?" I asked, examining him closely.

"About the same as I play." He stopped playing then and began looking around at the other instruments. He picked up the violin and twanged at the strings with his fingers.

"It sure isn't a Stradivarius, is it?" he laughed.

"No, and you're no Yehudi Menuhin either."

"Do you play?" he asked.

"No, I don't."

"What do you say we dance instead?" he suggested.

"I don't dance either, sorry. I better go and find my date."
I waggled my fingers and left. I got a glass of punch from the
serving table to make myself look at home and watched
Peacock Alley for the Englishman to leave. I had decided it
wasn't Etherington. Either the bride or groom here was
English. There were dozens of accents around, speaking in that
loud way that sounds like showing off to North Americans.
When the man came into the hall, a small group accosted him,
calling him by the name Herbie. I took this as *prima facie*
evidence he was not guilty and slipped back into the music
room for a closer search.

Like the Great Hall, this room was large but didn't offer that
many hiding spots. The violin wasn't behind either of the big
palms in the corners. It wasn't concealed behind the volumi-
nous folds of the brocade drapes, which would have been a
perfect hiding spot, if Victor had only realized they never
closed the drapes. I climbed over the velvet rope that cuts the
instruments off from the tourists, and determined that the violin
wasn't in the piano bench. Why couldn't he have put it in some
easy-to-get-at place like the piano bench? There were even a
few loose sheets of music that could have covered it.

There weren't many other places. The harp stood a few
yards to the left of the piano, accompanied by a little stool
upholstered in velvet. There was a cello on a stand closeby; it
had a chair with a back for the player. The piano's lid was
closed, and the violin was set at its end. Had Victor had time
to lift the lid of the grand piano and stick the violin in on top
of the piano strings? Was that why it sounded out of tune?

I picked up the violin to place it on the floor. It was propped
on its rather shabby case. I lifted the case, and was surprised by
its weight. I gave it a little shake. My heart went into nervous
palpitations as I realized what Victor had done. He had chosen
the most obvious place in the world to hide a violin. He had
simply put it in the violin case and propped the other violin on
top of the case as it had set for decades.

Sean had even picked up the violin and asked me if it was the
Strad, but he hadn't thought to pick up the case. Of course, I
could be wrong. It could be only some other old instrument the
castle owned kept here for convenience. I looked over my

shoulder. The hall was empty, but someone might come along at any moment. I took the violin case, opened the lid, and saw an undistinguished old violin with three strings broken. A spare put aside and forgotten.

Disappointed, frustrated, and becoming angry, I went to the chair beside one of the potted palms and sat down to think. It had to be here. It just *had* to. I glanced at the long-case clock still reading seven-fifteen, but it had a glass front, like the one in the Grand Hall. I looked again. The glass front had a gilt pattern of closely crossed lines forming small diamonds. The glass itself was dimmed from age. I rose like a zombie and went to the clock. You really couldn't see anything through the patterned glass. Even the pendulum was almost invisible.

My fingers trembled as I took hold of the knob and pulled the door open. There on the shadowed floor of the case, propped beside the unmoving pendulum sat a violin. I lifted it out and darted back to the chair by the palm where I wouldn't be seen from the hall if anyone peeked in. I'd never seen a Stradivarius in my life before, but I knew I was looking at one now. This was no ordinary instrument; it was an *objet d'art*. It felt perfectly balanced in my hands, and glowed a soft orangey-red where the "magical" varnish had mellowed. I didn't need the evidence of the ebony insets in the shape of a cluster of grapes to know this was a Stradivarius, but, of course, they confirmed that it was the Carpani Strad. The hairs on my arms lifted in homage to its perfection. For one moment, I suffered a peculiar atavistic attack of covetousness. I wanted to keep it. How much stronger must Victor's impulse have been? He had wanted one of these all his life and was one of the few men in the country who could do it justice. And who should such an object belong to if not to someone who could play it?

But how to smuggle it out? I darted to the grand piano, removed the unstrung violin from its case and took the case to my chair. I put the Stradivarius in the case, closed the lid and fastened it. My next thought was to get it out of here and home. Getting it out could prove the hardest part. There was a guard at the entrance, even for a wedding, and he'd take a dim view of someone walking out with part of the castle's furnishings. The other way out was the exit at the end of the hall by the lockers. In the exultant excitement of the moment that amounted almost to a frenzy, I didn't think of more practical moves such as calling the police or even a taxi. I just wanted to take the violin and run.

Running would only call attention to myself, and my aim was to get out as quietly as possible, so I did the next best thing. I walked out nonchalantly, carrying the violin case in my hand and even stopped to nod and smile to a few guests. Luck was with me. The guard wasn't at the door. He should have been, but a guard has to attend to nature's functions like anyone else, and for a few crucial minutes, the door was unguarded. I walked out unimpeded into the bright lights that shone on the castle so that it didn't even seem dark. It wasn't until I had walked beyond the bright lighting that I realized I should have called a cab. The dark spaces between those areas illuminated by street lights were long and menacing. I hurried past the dark spots, peering over my shoulder and caught my breath beneath the lamp standards.

I'd have to wait for a bus, but Toronto was relatively safe especially in respectable areas like this. I crossed the road and started to run for no particular reason except that I could no longer confine myself to normal behavior. I had to release some of the adrenaline that coursed through my veins, and shouting didn't seem like a very good idea.

There were cars passing by, quite a few of them, but this wasn't Maine. I had conquered the small-town habit of thinking I was going to know people I met on the street. My heart gave a lurch when a white Corvette sped past, but of course it wasn't Victor. A young couple was inside. I hardly glanced at the silver-gray Monte Carlo as it cruised by me a moment later. It couldn't be Sean—he was in custody. The man, the only person in the car, did have a head the shape of Sean's but it wasn't wearing a western hat. I hustled on, peering into the shadows as I went, and still keeping an eye on the silver Monte Carlo. Why was it slowing down? The corner didn't have a stop sign.

The car performed a U-turn and began speeding back toward me. Alarm quickly soared to outright panic. This was too much coincidence. I stopped dead in my tracks when the car began slowing down just a few yards from me. When it came to a full stop, I took to my heels, running back toward Casa Loma. But just before I turned, I got one quick glimpse of Sean's head emerging from the door. He was moving swiftly, and his expression went beyond sinister. He looked positively lethal. He *was* lethal—an escaped kidnapper and murderer for all I knew.

I ran as fast as my legs would carry me. The Casa Loma was only a block away. I could make it—but already the sound of hastening footfalls was gaining on me. My high heels, my clinging dress, and the violin case bumping against my body all slowed me down. And of course there wasn't a single pedestrian on the street. Cars sped by unaware of my predicament. He overtook me within half a block. I felt his large hand close over my shoulder in a powerful grip. He turned me around and leveled a cold, hard glare at me. "Why do I get the feeling you're trying to avoid me?" he asked ironically.

"Let go of me or I'll scream bloody murder."

He looked up and down the vacant street and smiled contentedly. I opened my mouth and emitted a blood-curdling scream. I heard it reverberate futilely in the air around me. Sean gave a grunt of amusement. "Save your breath. You'll need it." At this veiled threat, my heart leapt to my throat.

He gripped my upper arm in a vice hold and dragged me, loudly protesting, bucking and kicking, back to the Monte Carlo. I noticed he had left the door hanging open in his rush to catch me. At the car, he said, "I'll take this," and tossed the violin onto the seat of the car.

I made one more effort to get away. I tried to wrench free, but his fingers were like metal clamps on my arm. Fear rose up in a wave, a palpable, tangible thing when he shoved me toward the open car door. "How did you escape?" I asked.

"You heard about that, did you? Or was it you who tipped them off?" As he spoke, I dug in my heels and tried to resist. It took him about thirty seconds to pry me loose. I just had time for one final holler before I was flung onto the front seat, missing the violin case by a fraction of an inch.

He was in beside me. The motor was still running—all he had to do was put the car in gear and roar off. He was driving too fast for me to fling the door open and jump out. As he drove, he darted quick, angry looks at me.

"Well, was it you?"

"I don't know what you're talking about," I claimed bravely, but my shaking voice betrayed my fear, and my fingers were trembling. I crossed my arms to hide my panicky condition and thought furiously. How long would it take for Ronald to phone the apartment and discover I was missing? Would he come pelting over to see what had happened, or would he think I'd taken a sleeping pill as he'd suggested and decide to let me rest till morning? The police! At least they knew Sean had escaped. They must be looking for him, and they'd know what car he had rented. How had he got his car? He'd have been taken to the station in the police cruiser.

"The cops were waiting for me when I got back to the hotel as you apparently know," he said.

"Then how did you escape?"

"I didn't. I just did a bit of fast talking. They didn't have anything on me. Bad P.R., arresting an American and holding him with no evidence. I started yelling for the American Consul, and before you could say Jack Robinson they let me go."

Was it possible he had talked them into releasing him after what I'd told Marven? Or was this yet another lie? "They're probably having you followed," I said.

"Not now. I managed to lose them about half an hour ago. When I didn't find you in the apartment, I had a pretty good idea where to look. Did you know the Strad was there all along?"

"No, I just figured it out tonight." I was answering carefully, hoping to keep Sean calm, hoping to come up with a plan. He didn't seem terribly hostile, not yet anyway. But the very fact that he'd been "in" the apartment told me he had Victor's key. And there was no way he could have gotten it except from Victor.

"What were you planning to do with it?" he asked.

"Take it home. Call the police."

"Wouldn't it have made more sense to call them before you left the Casa Loma? Even before you left the apartment," he added.

"Yes, I guess it would."

"Of course, if you never had any intention of letting the cops know you'd found it . . ." He let it hang and snatched one quick look at me from the corner of his eye as he roared around a corner doing about seventy miles an hour.

"Why would I do that?"

"It's worth a lot of money."

"Not to me, it isn't. I just wanted the papers to announce it was found, so you—they'd let Victor go."

Sean didn't mention my slip, but I knew he'd noticed it. "Where's Ronald?" he asked suddenly.

"Out with some friends. Why?"

"When you stood me up, I thought maybe he was the cause."

"Where are we going?"

"To your place. A shame to let those two steaks go to waste. I didn't bring my pyjamas. I figured they'd just be in the way."

That was when the panic began getting out of control. I could almost taste it, bitter and burning at the back of my throat, making me weak and breathless. The talk so far had been very low key, not what I'd expected at all, but now he was going to get his revenge. He had the Strad, he had Victor and Victor's money and he had me. All he wanted was revenge. And there was nothing to prevent his getting it. He had evaded the police. Ronald was out somewhere with friends. He was going to take me back to the apartment . . . Beads of perspiration gathered on my brow and my fingers. I heard my shallow breathing in the closed car.

CHAPTER 16

My mind soon turned to escape—preferably before we reached the apartment. The blur of buildings and street lights told me we were going too fast to jump out. I thought Sean knew what I had in mind. He kept to the inner lane which made getting out in the traffic nearly as dangerous as staying with him. He rushed all the orange lights and once leapt through on a light that had just turned red. The time to make my bolt would be after we stopped. With luck on my side, there'd be some other people in the parking garage at the apartment; with divine providence, some of those people might be policemen. Or Ronald.

When we entered the garage, there was nothing but silent rows of dully gleaming cars and long shadowy aisles leading to the service elevators. Sean took a good look around before he got out. In all the excitement, it hadn't occurred to me that he might have a gun. And if he did, I could forget trying to bolt. I wanted to discover if he had one and peered for suspicious bulges in his clothing. It was impossible to tell by his lumpy jacket whether he carried a concealed weapon, but at least he didn't have one in his hand. I'd make a run for it as soon as the car stopped.

He parked so close to the other car on my side that I couldn't get my door open. He had done it on purpose, I knew by the smug set of his lips. This wily maneuver convinced me that he was too experienced to be walking around without a gun. I had to jiggle over and get out by his door while he stood waiting, watching closely.

He put on his hat and said, "You carry the violin."

I took it from him, he clamped a menacing hand on my arm, and we walked swiftly toward the elevator—the service elevator to lessen the likelihood of company. I uttered a silent prayer that when the elevator arrived, someone would be in it, a man, or men. It was already there, empty and waiting. My next and last hope was the hallway when we got out.

Sean stood behind me as we rode silently up in the elevator. I expected every minute that he'd do something—attack me with either lustful or other intent. And if he did, all I had for protection was my little evening purse and the Stradivarius violin worth a fortune. Not that that would have stopped me, but it was too fragile to do any good. There was no hope of the elevator stopping on the way up. Anyone using it would be going down to the garage. I kept picturing the hallway of the seventeenth floor, my last hope. *Please God, make there be someone in the hallway.*

When the elevator door rattled open, I looked into a perfectly empty stretch of corridor with rows of closed doors along either wall. Maybe if I screamed . . . I opened my lips. Sean heard my intake of breath and clamped his hand over my mouth. He dragged me along to Victor's door. At the door, he pulled out the key he'd taken from Victor and waited for me to go in before him. When I didn't he gave me a shove. Those two little inches of metal were as good as a confession that he'd kidnapped my uncle. I wondered what he'd done with the key ring and all Victor's other keys.

It was a strange feeling, the usual security of home all mixed up with the sheer terror of being here under duress with a dangerous criminal. But at least it was home. I knew the apartment more thoroughly than Sean did. Maybe I could find a weapon.

Before any concrete plan occurred to me, he tossed his head toward the violin case and said, "Let's have a look at it."

I put the case on the coffee table and opened it while quickly scanning the room for a weapon. The ash tray, close at hand, wasn't heavy enough. "So this is what all the fuss and bother was about," he said, lifting the violin, turning it around this way and that as though he'd never seen it before in his life. Maybe he hadn't; maybe Etherington had done the procuring, and I knew he'd handled the exchange. "Fuss and bother" struck me as a mild description of what Victor and I had been through, but then we probably rated low on his scale of victims.

While he was looking at the violin, the phone rang. Ronald! It was time for his call. I looked at Sean, waiting for him to decide whether he was going to let me answer. "If that's the boyfriend, tell him to get his keyster over here, fast. Tell him you've got the violin. That should do it."

I heard this order with delighted surprise. My incipient love for Ronald hadn't reached that unfathomable stage where I would sacrifice my life for his. Two against one gave me a fighting chance at least. Sean lifted the receiver and held it halfway between his ear and my own. We both heard Ronald say, "Hi, did you have a good sleep?"

My words came out in a strangled whisper. "Ronald, come right over. I found the Stradivarius."

"What! Where? How?" The questions came gushing out in an excited babble.

"Come right over," I repeated just before Sean reached out a finger and cut us off.

"That should do it," he smiled. But it wasn't a real smile, more a baring of teeth. There was nothing pleasant in it.

"Now what'll we have to drink? Coffee or beer?" was his next question.

A kitchen had knives—which Sean would soon wrestle out of my hand and quite possibly turn against me. "Nothing for me," I said.

He gave me a mocking smile. "Has something put you off your feed?"

This wasn't the moment to risk a smart ass answer. He went to the bar and poured a shot of Scotch into a glass. He sipped it like that, with no ice and no water, in the English way. While he sipped, his eyes seldom left me. "Was it you, or was it the boyfriend who sent the cops to the hotel?" he asked after about a minute of that silent, sinister staring.

"That's the second time you've asked that. I still don't know what you're talking about."

"The pictures were stolen from your purse. It doesn't make any sense for Strathroy to call attention to those pictures. Even if he knew, and if he gave them to you, he wouldn't be eager for Marven to know about them."

"Why not?"

There was a feeling of tiptoeing on eggs during this exchange. I didn't want to get Sean in a fit of fury before Ronald came, and he seemed to be just as edgy and secretive as I was. "If you trust him so much, how come you went alone to pick up the Strad?"

"Ronald was busy. I just decided at the last minute to go. Never mind about Ronald. What are you going to do about Victor?"

"I don't know. That depends on Victor."

"Sean, you won't let Etherington kill him!"

"No, I won't," he agreed, but diffidently. "Sure you don't want a shot of this stuff? It's real good Scotch."

"It should be. It's old enough to vote. Maybe I'll have a bit of that Irish Cream."

It was an unreal quarter of an hour we spent waiting for Ronald to come. Sean had two neat Scotches, and I had two shots of Irish Cream. The bottle might have been capable of knocking him out if he'd ever stopped staring at me long enough to get a crack at him. I could tell by the intense glow in his eyes that he was doing some deep scheming. Whatever it was caused a pleat to form between his brows, and the gouges at either side of his moustache to deepen. He seemed content to just think, and so I remained silent and thought too.

"The pictures were stolen from your purse," he had said. An odd way to say he'd stolen them. Would he kill Victor or not? If it was an identification he was worried about, then he'd have to kill me and Ronald too, and surely Sean wasn't a mass murderer. He'd just tie us up and make a fast getaway.

When I figured it was nearly time for Ronald to arrive, I risked a question that had been bothering me ever since Marven told me this man wasn't Sean Bradley. "Who are you?" I asked.

"My name, you mean?"

"Yes."

He hesitated a moment then answered, "John. John Weiss."

"Where are you from?"

"The west."

"From North Platte?"

"North of there. My dad does own a hardware store. I worked there summers when I was in high school. I stick as close to the truth as I can. No point complicating life by claiming a profession you can't fake. You never know when you might meet somebody who can blow your cover wide open."

"You were wise to stick to two-by-fours," I snipped before I realized the danger of angering him. But he didn't seem angry. "How did you get mixed up in this business—I mean this specific business of Victor and the violin?"

"You mean what's a nice guy like me doing in a business like this?" He laughed. "I've been chasing the Carpani loot for months, ever since Etherington lifted it from the contessa's villa. The violin is the least interesting thing in it, but it surfaced first so it might lead to the rest of the stuff. They try to get rid of it all at the same time—usually in different countries so word doesn't get around. That's why it's so important to certain people that it shouldn't be found and identified. I'm a specialist," he said proudly. Pride in stealing previously-stolen goods was as bizarre as the rest of that bizarre night.

The door buzzer sounded, and I looked at Sean for permission to answer it. The doorman often let Eleanor and Ronald up without announcing them. "Let him in. And let me do the talking. If he tries anything . . . But no, I don't think Ronald will sully his lily whites by trying to sock me." He gave an ironical little laugh and followed me to the door.

I opened it, and Ronald came charging in. He stopped dead when he saw Sean. For a minute I had a very real fear that he was going to turn tail and run. But Sean gave him an oily smile that seemed to set his fears at rest, and he came reluctantly into the living room.

"Surprise!" Sean smiled and pointed at the Strad.

Introductions seemed irrelevant, but in case Ronald wasn't aware who he was dealing with, I said, "This is Sean Bradley, Ron." I tried to give him a mute warning by frowning and staring at him. Just what warning I didn't know myself, but I wanted him to know at least that Sean wasn't the disinterested friend he would probably pretend to be. Why had he called Ronald here anyway? Ronald apparently interpreted my grimaces to mean he wasn't to ask any close questions as to why Sean was here when he should have been in jail.

Ronald looked at the violin, then at Sean, at me, then all around the apartment. "Is this it? The stolen violin?" he asked and went to look at it. "Yes, I can see it is. The grapes . . . Where did you find it?" He threw the question midway between Sean and myself.

Sean answered. "Cassie found it at the Casa Loma."

"It was in the bottom of the long-case clock in the music room, practically in plain view all the time," I added.

"This is wonderful!" Ronald exclaimed. "Congratulations. Well, have you called the police?"

"Not yet," Sean said.

"What are you waiting for?"

Maybe now we'd hear just what John Weiss had in mind, for the violin and us, and Victor. "You mean to use it to get Victor back?" Ron asked, frowning at me.

"The trouble is, we don't know who to deal with," Sean said, as though at a loss.

"Yes, I see your dilemma." Ron's eyes took on the same scheming look Sean's had worn earlier and still wore, though slightly diminished.

I watched this farce for half a minute and decided there was no point in it. "Surely *you* have some idea, Sean?" I said. My tone, I trust, left no doubt as to my meaning.

Ronald scowled behind Sean's back and began to propitiate him. "She's a little confused," he smiled. "There was a bit of a fracas here this afternoon, Sean. I imagine Cassie told you." Sean nodded. "We heard about your arrest." Then he turned to me. "Obviously you were mistaken about Sean, Cassie. The police wouldn't have released him if he'd been criminally involved in your uncle's disappearance. What is your involvement, Sean? RCMP?"

"That's right," Sean said.

I stared in utter incredulity. Sean—John—a policeman? I hastily considered the past days, and saw that this was indeed

possible. I felt as though a weight had lifted from my heart. I
wanted to laugh and shout for sheer relief.

When Sean spoke, his western twang had diminished
noticeably, though he still didn't sound exactly like a Canadian. "When the crime goes beyond provincial boundaries,
they call us in. Of course, this one's international."

"The Mounties are like the FBI in the States," Ronald
explained for my edification.

"When they picked me up, I had to reveal myself to the local
fuzz."

"And that's why Marven released you," Ronald nodded.
"You two weren't working together before tonight, I take it?"

"Too many cooks spoil the broth," Sean answered.

Ron said, "I see," and gave me an intense look that told me
nothing.

"I don't see," I said bluntly. "If you're a Mountie, why
didn't you arrest Etherington when he sold the thing to
Victor?"

"Etherington's just a gofer," Sean said. "We wanted to
catch the main man. The Strad is a very small part of the loot
from the Carpani villa," he continued to Ronald. "There were
artworks and jewelry worth roughly three million taken at the
same time. We followed Etherington instead of Mazzini the
day of the sale. It proved to be a mistake."

"You might say that," I agreed. My voice didn't sound as
ironical as I hoped. Disbelief robbed it of emphasis. I tried to
make some sense of Sean's story and found a dozen holes in it.
Obviously Etherington had followed Victor, so if Sean had
been following Etherington, he'd know where Victor was too.
And why had he lured Ronald over here? Why was he telling
us all this?

"Are you saying it wasn't Etherington who kidnapped
Victor?" Ronald asked.

The scheming look was back full force on Sean's face but
overlaid with a self-conscious sheepishness. "No, it was
Etherington all right. Actually it was my colleague who
handled that end of it," Sean said. "The little swarthy guy in
the dark suit—you might have noticed him, Cassie. He lost
Etherington."

"I see," Ronald said again and nodded again.

I didn't nod, but I saw yet another gaping hole in Sean's story. He and the little swarthy man had been together at the Casa Loma. And it wasn't Etherington they'd been following; it was Victor.

Ronald finally woke up to the fact that there was something highly irregular in Sean's behaviour and said, "Why are you telling me all this?"

"You and your mother are about the best friends Mazzini has here in Toronto. I figure Victor will have them contact you when the time comes for him to be sprung. That should be about two minutes after we announce that the Carpani Strad has been found. That's the only reason they've been holding him—to keep him quiet."

"Don't be ridiculous! My uncle will contact me!" I said.

"They'll want to deal with a man," Sean said, as though it were self-evident. He and Ron exchanged a smug, superior little masculine smile.

"That's true," Ron agreed. "And you want me to try to set up something to catch Etherington when the swap is made, Victor for the violin?"

"Exactly." Now he had no interest in the fictitious "main man." Etherington was suddenly his quarry.

"How do you figure they'll want to do it?" Ron asked.

"If they've got any smarts at all, they'll blindfold Mazzini, drive him out to some spot on the edge of town that's deserted around midnight. They'll want to put a few miles between their hiding place and the drop. Some suburban shopping mall parking lot—something like that. Good, easy getaway and not too much concealment in case you brought along the fuzz. Quick access to a good highway, too."

"They'll want me to go alone, I suppose?" Ronald asked.

"For sure. And they'll make you get out of your car and go to theirs. They'll be parked in shadows with their lights off. What you've got to do is make damned sure Mazzini is alive before you hand over the violin."

"How come you're so ready to hand over the violin?" I asked. "It's not Victor you're worried about. It's that damned chunk of wood," I said, pointing to the Strad.

"I'm interested in both."

"Naturally he doesn't intend for the kidnappers to get

away," Ron explained. "You'll have the police hiding nearby, ready to cut them off as they leave—right, Sean?"

"Ronald, don't be a dope!" I warned. "You'll end up with a bullet in your head and so will Victor. Once the police go swarming in . . ."

"No, no, there won't be any shooting," Sean promised. "Not till we've got Mazzini and Ron here safely out of the picture. We'll let Etherington and company get away—or think they have. They'll head for the 401, the trans-Canada Highway. Wouldn't make any sense to head any other way. They don't want to get bogged down in suburbs. They're not local folks, you see, and might spend hours driving around cul de sacs and crescents and whatnot. A homing pigeon could get lost in those suburbs."

"And you could lose Etherington if he did go that way," I pointed out.

"He might lose himself," Sean explained. "I won't lose him. Ron's going to stick this little transmitter in the violin case for us," he said, holding up a little black thing about as big as a penny. "Me and Marven will be following with a scanning antenna. Directional—we'll home in on that sucker and follow him till we get him in some dark, deserted spot where we can take him without killing anybody. Then we'll recover the Strad and the money your uncle paid them and make him tell us where the rest of the Carpani loot is. The little problem is letting Etherington know we've got the violin."

"This is crazy. They'll kill Victor," I said. "He can identify them."

"No way," Sean said confidently. "They're not going to add murder one to their record. You murder a celebrity like Mazzini, you're buying big trouble. There's how many, Ron, something like twenty-five thousand cops in Toronto wanting to make a name for themselves? Then there's the Provincial Police and the Mounties. Jeez, they'd have to be nuts to go for murder one. They'll make the exchange all right and hope to make a getaway."

"I'm going to call Marven," I said.

Both Ronald and Sean went into shock. "You don't call the police in on a kidnapping, Cassie," Ronald explained. "That's always the first order the kidnappers give."

"You already got the police here, Ms. Newton," Sean reminded me. I hardly recognized this stranger with the new accent who suddenly took it into his head to call me Ms. Newton. "Like I said, too many cooks spoil the broth. If they see uniforms around, they'll hightail it out of there so fast your head'll spin. I don't plan to use the local fuzz. Greenhorns— they'd only gum up the works."

"You plan to go after Etherington by yourself?" Ron asked.

"I have to let Marven in on it now that he knows who I am, but I'm in charge. Just me and my colleague and Marven. That's plenty. I'll call Marven in later, after we hear from Etherington," Sean said. "The thing now is to let Etherington and his boss know we've got the violin."

"They'll take Victor's money and run once they hear you know they're the Carpani gang," I pointed out.

"Why should they when they think they can get the violin back as well?" Ronald asked. "It can still be sold to somebody else. Lots of people will knowingly buy stolen goods. Not everyone likes a public demonstration of his possessions like Victor. Don't you agree, Sean?"

"There's sheiks and Arabs out there that would buy Fort Knox if they could figure out a way to get it moved," Sean agreed. "Besides, there wouldn't be much publicity if the violin just disappeared. There wouldn't be pictures and all that. They'd have to wait a year or so. I guess the TV and radio will do for starters, to let them contact us. I hope our boys listen in and contact us before morning. I'd like to get this wrapped up before daylight. Guess the first thing is to call the media."

I sat, numb with dissatisfaction and disbelief while Sean phoned up the TV and radio stations. He made a special point of warning them to keep reporters away from the apartment. "Just announce that Victor Mazzini has been kidnapped and is being held for ransom. Not money, a Stradivarius violin stolen from the villa of the Contessa Carpani, in Cremona, Italy. It was a big robbery around New Year's this year. You must have something on file. Mazzini bought the thing. I know it's confusing, but just make the announcement." He argued with them but finally convinced them to make the report.

"The police just might be listening to the TV and radio, too," I mentioned.

"Can't be helped," Sean shrugged. "I've tipped Marven not to do anything without calling me first."

Then we turned on the TV and radio and just waited for the announcement.

CHAPTER 17

About two minutes after the local TV station ran the story on a special newsbreak, Marven called.

Sean took the call and admitted the story was true. He explained that we were waiting to hear from Etherington. "And remember, keep your boys off. I mean it, Marven. You send uniforms in to bugger up my show, and you'll be back walking a beat."

"If you think he'll call me, I'd better be at home," Ronald said.

"He'll call me," I said flatly.

"What do you think, Sean?" Ronald asked, ignoring me completely.

"Why don't you stick around for a while?"

It was a great satisfaction when the phone rang about ten minutes later, and a cultured English accent announced itself as being interested in the news report that the Carpani Strad had been found.

I answered the phone, but Sean put his ear to it, too, and Ronald hovered close enough that he could hear. Sean snatched the receiver from me and asked, "Are you ready for a deal?"

"I didn't call to discuss the weather."

"Put Mazzini on the line. We're not buying a corpse."

After about fifteen seconds of agonizing silence, Victor's unmistakable voice blared forth. "Cassie, are you there? Listen, this guy is nuts. If you found the Strad, don't give it to him. That's an order." His voice sounded thick, blurred with drugs or pain.

The English voice took control again. "Satisfied?" he asked.

Ron grabbed the receiver out of Sean's hand and exploded in a way that did him credit. "Listen, you creep, this is Ronald Strathroy speaking. If you so much as lay a finger on Mr. Mazzini, I personally will tear your guts out."

The caller hung up. "Oh jeez, Ron!" Sean complained with a grimace. "Now we'll have to wait forever for him to call back."

Ron ran his fingers through his hair. "I'm sorry. I lost my head. I was just afraid they'd hurt Victor. He's an old man. They *will* call back, won't they?"

"Who knows? They'll be afraid we've got a trace put on the line. I wonder . . . You gave him your name. Maybe he'll call you at your place."

"Do you think I should go home?" Ronald asked uncertainly.

Sean rubbed his chin and thought about it. "That might be best. I'll be here, in case they call back. You let me know right away if you hear from them."

"Of course. I'll make the arrangements if they call."

"Don't go to meet them alone, Ron," I said. Ronald spent his life on Bay Street. The most dangerous thing he ever did was hit a squash ball. Sean, on the other hand, could handle himself and maybe the kidnappers, too. "Sean, you could hide in the back seat."

"It's okay with me," Sean agreed. "You want me to tag along, Ron?"

"No, no. I can handle it," Ron said bravely. "Should I take the violin now? It'd save coming back."

"No, better leave it here," Sean said. "There's no saying Etherington caught your name. But you'd better take this, just in case." He reached in his jacket pocket and handed Ron a little snub-nosed revolver.

Ronald looked unhappy, but he left without the violin. Sean stayed behind, rubbing his chin. Then he zapped a laser-beam smile at me and shook my hand. "He fell for it!" he said jubilantly and laughing like a hyena.

I froze in position. Now what was he up to? "Fell for what?"

"The setup. What a dope! How did he ever have the wits to engineer this operation? Etherington must be the brains."

"Are you crazy? Do you still think Ronald Strathroy had anything to do with all this?"

"Everything. You don't believe it? That phone will ring within half an hour. It'll be Ron, calling for the Strad. He'll have arranged the swap, just like I told him. I could see he was adrift, not knowing how to get his butt out in one piece, so I gave him a little help. Did you notice how eager he was to get away, said he should go home and wait for the call? And how fast he was to grab the phone out of my hand, to let his pal know he was here, too, and that he wasn't under suspicion? It was as good as telling Etherington to sit tight till he could call him with instructions."

"You're nuts. You're way off base. You're going to send Ron out there alone to get himself killed."

"Oh, he won't really be alone. The place'll be crawling with cops. Especially the roads into the suburbs since he'll tell his friend we're only blocking access to the 401. He seemed to swallow it, that there'd only be me and Marven. That guy's sinfully gullible."

"But what if you're wrong? What if Ron's innocent?"

"I'm not wrong. And if I am, what I said about murder one still stands. They're not going to bump off your uncle just for the hell of it, and they're not going to kill Ronald, either. Etherington at least is a pro. He'd stick at murder."

"But if Ron is involved, he won't really put the bug in the violin case! He'll say it got broken or lost or something."

"Bug? Oh that. No, he won't use it of course, but it doesn't matter. Etherington will never get out of our sight. That was just to make him think it would be easy to get away. I'd better give Marven a call. I really don't want him sending marked cars over here to screw up the works."

He dialled Marven and spoke with no effort to hide his talk from me. "He took the bait. Did you get a trace on the incoming call? . . . Too bad, I figured there wasn't time when Strathroy scared his pal off. . . . Good! I have the violin, so he has to be in touch with me. This is it. We've got him, Fred."

He hung up, smiled, and patted his stomach. "We might have time to cook that steak and eat it if we hustle."

"I don't think so. First we'd have to find a cow and butcher it. Do you want an egg sandwich?"

"No steaks marinating? No wine breathing?" he chided. "If I eat another egg, I'll start cackling."

"A ham sandwich—or are you not into cannibalism?"

"Male Chauvinist Pig, right? You didn't like my leaving you out. I had to find some way to draw Strathroy in. You were the obvious one for Etherington to phone, but I used the myth that women are helpless critters to let Ron join the fun and games. Part of the trick of a sting is to make the illogical seem logical."

"Like making me think I came up with the idea of Victor buying a stolen Stradivarius, for instance?"

"You would have thought of it sooner or later."

"Not in ten years. Who's Betty Friske? I mean why was your little friend in the blue suit at her door?"

"I sent him—Gino. Betty's thinking of buying a life insurance policy from him. You got me wondering if the poor innocent woman might be involved somehow. She isn't—her only involvement is that Victor tried to put the bite on her for five thousand to buy the Strad. A loan only, and she would have obliged him, too, if he could sell her jewelry. But his stocks were up, so he didn't need it after all. He was selling his car and cottage to pay off the bank. You were lucky he didn't put his condo on the block."

"I've had a lot of occasion to thank Lady Luck lately."

His brows wriggled lecherously. "You and me both, Cassie. I thought you were just another airhead when I first met you. A real space cadet, but I see you've got grit. It took some guts to get into my hotel room and nick the pictures. It would have been even smarter if you hadn't dropped your comb—the little pink one with the broken handle."

I didn't believe him, but a quick search of my purse showed me it was missing. "I was kind of hoping you'd admit it. I gave you a couple of chances to unburden your black soul. When you went to the Casa Loma alone, I thought maybe you'd figured out it was Ron who set your uncle up. You did tell him you took the pictures from my room, didn't you?"

"Yes. I even invited him over. He must have thought about the locker, too, and stopped in on his way to the apartment to have a look for the Strad. I guess he unscrewed the bulb when he heard me coming. But he must have known Victor didn't hide it there since he was taken in the garage before he got to the apartment."

"They didn't know where he'd hidden it, or when. They searched the apartment and the cottage, too. They must have figured he handed the violin over to somebody."

"Imagine, Ronald Strathroy bopping me on the head. But how did he get into the apartment to rifle my purse?"

"He got Victor's key from Etherington."

"Of course."

"Never trust a guy that gets his fingers manicured professionally. He's weird, one way or the other. You should have come running to me for help. Begging for forgiveness. Promising me anything I wanted . . ."

"You shouldn't have given Ron a gun," I said to cut off this embarrassing fantasy.

"Blanks," he said curtly. "This one's got real bullets," he added and pulled a black pistol from his boot.

"Why don't you get into some more practical clothes?" he suggested. "That white thing will show up too well in the shadows."

My anger with Sean had shrunk to manageable irritation; the irritation evaporated like mist in the sun when he said that. "You mean I can go with you?"

"What's Sherlock Holmes without Dr. Watson?"

"What's a ham without grits?"

"Apple pie without cheese—a kiss without a squeeze?"

His long arms reached for me; his moustache attacked violently. The Mounties trained their men very well in the amorous arts. Two dozen or so questions were still waiting to be answered, but I let them wait and savored the experience of being attacked by an officer of the Royal Canadian Mounted Police. It was easy to imagine Sean's western hat as the traditional Mountie's Stetson. The jeans jacket and jeans gave way to scarlet tunic and navy jodhpurs, the cowboy boots to tall black Wellingtons, or whatever those calf-hugging boots were called.

A man in uniform was every bit as satisfying a fantasy as a worldweary intellectual. He kissed much better. No fooling around with sweet nothings in my ear. It was serious, nonstop kissing of an energetic and accomplished sort that left me reeling in abandonment when the phone rang.

"Square One, Mississauga, at midnight," Sean relayed after he hung up. "What the hell is Square One, Mississauga?"

"A shopping mall. Mississauga is a kind of urban sprawl west of Toronto," I smiled inanely. "What about the violin?"

"Ron's picking it up here. I'll put in the bug for him to take out. I'm meeting him down at the garage. Want to be waiting in the back seat of my car? It'll save time."

I got out of my dress and into jeans and a dark jersey while Sean phoned Marven and laid plans to trap Ron. Very detailed plans; they even had boats standing by at the edge of Lake Ontario. I was in the back seat of the Monte Carlo with a rain coat over my head when Sean handed over the violin to Ron, and as soon as Ron left, Sean had me hop into the front seat to direct him to Mississauga. He drove about ninety miles an hour in the city to make sure he was there before Ron. The other policemen were already in place.

"You know if Ron were really involved in this, he wouldn't have phoned you. He'd have done the whole thing behind your back. What makes you think he'll actually go to Square One?" He squealed around a corner, throwing me against the door, and as we straightened out, he answered.

"Why wouldn't he? He's playing the role of hero. His fingers would look clean if Etherington got away, and as far as he knows, Etherington *will* get away. That's the way we planned it, remember?"

"*You* planned it. When it blows up in your face, I want to be able to say 'I told you so.' Do you know why Ron got involved in all this?"

He leaned into the windshield and squeaked past an oncoming car with his knuckles turning white on the wheel. "Sure. He's in debt over his ears. He's siphoned thousands out of his clients' accounts at Graymar and had to cover his ass."

"How did you suspect him?"

"Ozone lady, you disappoint me. He had been to the Carpani villa, knew all about the treasures there, and had a few ideas about nicking them. He claimed to be in Montreal transacting business on a holiday when no business was done, and a check showed no Ronald Strathroy had a plane ticket. He was here, giving his friend Etherington a hand. He knew Victor would give his false teeth for a Strad and knew he could raise the dough."

"Sean! Watch out for that fire hydrant!" His wheels had roamed up over the curb, but at least there were no pedestrians on the sidewalk. After we had bumped back down to the road, I said, "I wonder how Ron ever got in touch with a crook like Etherington. His friends are all very respectable. More than respectable."

"Except for Etherington. Etherington owed him money. Something to do with buying on margin and having to cover or lose his down payment. I don't imagine Etherington is a brand new acquaintance. He's an old Oxford type—there the same time as Ron, actually. Etherington's fingers have proved sticky in the past. He's the guy I've been following—ever since a certain Raphael sketch turned up in Toronto last month. It was sold to a rich recluse-type collector who didn't ask too many questions, but the guy did show it to one expert who recognized it and reported it. I guess the buyer had a streak of Victor in him somewhere. He just couldn't keep it to himself."

"You mean you've been here ever since May and knew all along that Etherington had my uncle! But why didn't you . . . That light was *red*, Sean!"

"It was orange. That's what orange lights are for, so you don't have to stop when you're going fast. About your uncle, I didn't know *where* he had him. Etherington was living in the Delta Inn. Why do you think I'm there? He checked out Wednesday. He'd moved two or three times already. That's how guys like him operate. He's holed up somewhere, probably not in a hotel now—too public. He didn't have the rest of the loot at the inn. I've searched his room a dozen times. Strathroy wouldn't have it. They've rented some place, probably in the country, and that's where they've got Victor."

"It seems a dirty trick to kidnap Victor after he paid them good money for the violin."

"It was that unexpected stop at Bitwell's that threw them into a tailspin. The Royal Conservatory—a good place for an expert on musical instruments to hang out, and the grim look on Victor's face when he came out probably told Etherington your uncle knew the truth. They had to keep him quiet, or they'd never be able to unload the rest of the Carpani loot. Etherington looks like a rich Englishman. His M.O. is to sell the stuff privately, pretending it's family heirlooms he's obliged to sell. He gets more for it that way than fencing it. Etherington panicked, I imagine, and just hustled Victor into a car. And then discovered he didn't have the violin. I wonder where they're hiding him. That I couldn't find out. Should I have turned there?"

"No, straight ahead." I gave up the battle of trying to get him to slow down and drive on the road. "Why couldn't you find where they're hiding him? You were following Etherington—and Victor. Where did you lose them?"

"Gino lost his quarry. I stayed behind to strike an acquaintance with Victor's niece."

"You left with Gino."

"All right!" he said, through clenched teeth. "You don't let a guy put up a good front, do you? We lost them at Casa Loma. When we got there, both their cars were empty—Victor's and Etherington's. We figured they'd both gone in. Gino went looking for Etherington; I followed Victor. When we got out, Etherington's car was gone. I stuck with the white Corvette. There were three damned white Corvettes there that day. Can you believe it, three white Corvettes? And a guy with silver hair got into one of them. I followed him—to the 401. At the turnoff I got close enough to see his license number and realized I'd goofed.

"I followed this guy who wasn't Victor, and Gino was supposed to look for Etherington. He didn't find him. Of course, later we figured Etherington knew it was too hard to kidnap a guy in broad daylight and had driven to Victor's apartment to take him, probably at gun point, when he got out. It was during that time they were apart that Victor ditched the Stradivarius, and Etherington had no idea where. That's why Ron's been looking in the apartment and the cottage, and probably why he was breaking into the locker when you were there.

"Meanwhile, Victor wasn't sure whether he was still being

followed or not, and decided to confuse Etherington by putting his empty violin case in the locker. We weren't entirely positive how innocent Victor was—how much he was paying for the Strad, and whether he knew it was hot. It seemed like a good idea to be on friendly terms with the family. Especially when the family was so darned pretty," he added as a sop.

"Let's try to keep her that way. That means don't cross any more double lines." He pulled an inch to his own side. "Gino's a Mountie too?"

"He's my assistant."

It was a pretty good story. I was convinced, but a few loose ends were still sticking out, here and there. "Who searched the apartment the night Victor disappeared?"

"Had to be Ron. He left Etherington in charge of your uncle for obvious reasons—he didn't want Victor to see him."

"Do you suppose Eleanor knows what's going on?"

"Eleanor doesn't know enough to come in out of the rain. All that lady knows is spending money. That's half of Ron's problem. She wouldn't have blurted out that it was the Carpani Strad if she'd been in on it. Till then, we hadn't tied Etherington to Strathroy. They were never seen together. I've looked into all Etherington's pals. We knew he had an accomplice. It was a gift from the gods when the accomplice turned out to be my competition," he grinned.

"I bet he mentioned the cottage on purpose to send me running up there and get me out of the way. He'd already been there himself and knew I wouldn't find anything. He never kept such close track of me before. Boy, he's been camping on the doorstep ever since Victor vanished."

"The greater mystery is how you could let that cashmere creep near you."

"I'm not allergic to cashmere."

"Real men don't wear little striped suits—that's for pencil pushers. But we'll call him a man tonight, since a Mountie always has to get his man. As soon as I get my man, I'll go after my woman," he promised and smiled like a satyr.

He was so smitten he nearly missed the turnoff to Mississauga. A driver should keep his eyes on the road and at least one hand on the wheel.

CHAPTER 18

"Highway 10, that's it," Sean said and turned left. "Square One Mall will be three major roads down, on your right, according to Marven. A lot of roads for his men to cover. There's two big highways to the south, the 401 north, and any number of little roads. I hope they nab him before he leaves the parking lot."

"You promised there wouldn't be shooting!"

"I promised we wouldn't shoot your uncle."

"Where are we going to be?"

"If he gets away, he'll head south. A big lake there, Lake Ontario, with a yacht club every mile, and another whole country to lose himself in on the other side of it. Grab a boat, and he's away. That's why we can't let him out of the parking lot."

"But you don't mean to be so far from the action?" I objected.

"No, I don't, but you'll be in this car with the motor running a hundred or so yards south of Square One."

I let him dream on. The spread of the shopping center, its neon lights proclaiming it the heart of suburbia, soon came into view on the right. There was a scattering of cars from the night cleaning staff and guards. It was too far away to distinguish whether Ron's Mercedes was among them, and we didn't know what Etherington would be driving. Sean coasted into the shadows of a patch of trees some yards beyond. There was an anticipatory, febrile glitter in his eyes and a smile lifting his moustache.

"They shouldn't be there for another quarter of an hour, but I wouldn't want to be late for this date. Wish me luck," he said and pulled the gun from his boot. With this engine of death dangling from his fingers, he reached out, scratched my lips with his moustache, and left.

I let him get a few yards back toward the shopping mall before I followed after him. I went to the edge of the parking lot and hunkered down behind some bushes to wait. My fantasy life involved much danger, none of it quite as clear and present and scarey as what faced me now. Many nights, my head comfortably resting on goose feathers, I single-handedly trapped half a dozen spies and traitors. I highly recommend this fantasy way of getting your thrills. The real thing is not only unpleasant but actually has its tedious moments.

After about ten minutes, my legs muscles went into cramps, and I had to do a bit of careful stretching, or I wouldn't be in condition to trip up any criminals who came my way. I spent the ten minutes looking at the nearly empty parking lot. If Marven had a host of men anywhere near, they were invisible. There wasn't a living thing on that lot except a cat out on the prowl. Several cars shot past on the highway behind me, each one causing a lurch of frightened hope.

Finally, one of them slowed down and turned in. It was a big, dark, squarish car and looked like an older Ford LTD. I could only see one head in it, a man's head. Its lights were suddenly switched off, and the car coasted to a stop, not close to the mall entrance, as I expected, but closer to the spot where I was crouched. Of course, it was darker here, and as I looked around, I noticed I had by chance hidden myself at the farthest distance from any parked cars. I crouched lower while my heart went into high gear. The car wasn't close enough to cause any real panic. There was about ten yards between us, and the man didn't get out of the car. He left the motor running. The car was too far away for me to determine whether the driver wore a moustache.

About four minutes later, another car on the highway slowed down and nosed into the lot. I recognized Ron's Mercedes. It drove toward the parked LTD and pulled in front of it. Ron got out stiffly, looked all around, and went back to the other car. He wasn't carrying the violin case—already things weren't going as they were supposed to. The window was opened and Ron leaned down to talk to the driver. I strained my ears, but heard only the low rumble of voices. The driver got out, opened the back door and he and Ron hauled Victor out onto the pavement. He was trussed up somehow and was so inert I feared he was dead.

Every atom of my being urged me forward to investigate, but self-preservation, that strongest of all instincts, held me quiet. The men continued talking in low tones. In a moment Etherington would leave, Ron would be arrested and I could rush to Victor. I could endure another minute after all the hours already endured. So I waited and watched and tried to hear the low conversation. It was a louder exclamation from Etherington that alerted me to danger. "What the hell is that?" he demanded.

I followed the direction of his gaze and saw a dog, a stray mutt that had escaped its leash or been let out in the concealment of darkness for its exercise. "Just a stray mutt," Ron answered.

It looked like a black mongrel with some Labrador blood, and went toward them, wagging its tail to indicate friendship. It began sniffing at Victor. Etherington lifted his foot and kicked it away. The dog was no hero. It ran yelping—straight to me. First I tried to pray it away. It stood there, tail wagging, yapping. Perspiration beaded on my brow. It would be only a matter of seconds till Etherington decided he should investigate. Already he was casting suspicious glances toward my bushes. "Go away. Bad dog," I growled in a low voice. The dog barked louder.

"There's something there!" I heard Etherington say. "Jesus, is it the cops?"

I couldn't hear Ron's answer, but it sounded impatient and off-putting.

The dog, an utter demon of persistence, ran playfully halfway to Etherington then back to me as though urging him to investigate what he had found. I hunkered lower behind the bushes. Etherington wouldn't come. Why should he? If I were a cop, this would be the last place he'd approach. And even if he did, Sean was somewhere nearby. But where?

When Etherington turned and began to stride purposefully toward me, my whole body congealed in horror. This couldn't be happening. But it was. Not only was he coming straight at me, he was carrying a gun in his hand. The pale moon overhead cast menacing shadows on his face when he stared down behind the bushes. It was the face from the pictures, a somewhat dissolute face but with a suggestion of decayed nobility in the haughty brow, the wedge of a sculptured nose above the brush moustache.

He didn't speak. He just make a beckoning motion with the gun while the dog barked his pleasure. Silently, I rose from behind the bushes, my eyes never leaving the muzzle that was pointed straight at me. He was going to kill me. No, Sean said he was a pro. He'd stick at murder. Strangely, it was Ron who spoke.

"Cassie! What are you doing here?"

A malevolent smiled twitched Etherington's lips. "Yes, Cassie, what *are* you doing here? As if I didn't know." He looked suspiciously at Ron. "No point leaving loose ends," he added.

"Don't shoot her!" Ron ordered, but I noticed he didn't come forward to help me.

Etherington continued motioning with his gun, urging me toward the car. I saw Victor on the ground, and bent over him, trying to determine if he was alive or dead. And if they'd already killed Victor . . . The voices continued arguing.

"Don't be ridiculous," I heard Ron shout.

I watched in rising panic as Etherington turned on him in a vicious attack. First a powerful crack over the head with the butt of his gun, then a fist rammed into his stomach. Ronald crumbled to the ground in a heap beside Victor. And as if that wasn't bad enough, Etherington next turned his violent anger on me. "Get in," he ordered grimly. "You might come in handy yet."

"I—" I looked helplessly at Victor and Ronald, one all trussed up, the other sprawled in an inert mass.

"Now," Etherington growled. I moved toward the LTD. "The other car," he said, pushing me toward Ron's Mercedes, the driver's side. I crawled in; Etherington was right after me.

It seemed I should have been able to stop him in some way. He had to not only drive, but keep the gun on me. What deterred my attempt was that he paid more attention to me and the gun than to the driving. The car leapt forward and hurtled down the length of the parking lot. I had thought he'd turn around and leave the way he'd arrived. He was soon going too fast for me to jump out. Did he know some exit that Sean didn't know about? Oh, God, was he going to escape with me as hostage?

We reached the end of the lot, and I discovered that Etherington didn't know of any secret exit. He was just investigating. There was a barrier too high to jump. He whipped around in a perilous U-turn that sent me slamming against the door, and he began driving back. The parking lot had sprung to life. We met cars coming toward us—three I think. One set of headlights was dead in our tracks. I braced myself for the sickening clang of metal on metal, and lifted my arms to protect my face. The oncoming lights veered to the left, missing us by inches.

I swallowed my heart and looked through the windshield again. Behind us, tires were squealing as the cop cars performed their U-turns and came after us. Farther down the lot, men were running and cars were moving. The cars of the cleaning staff had either been conscripted, or the cops had slid a batch of their own unmarked cars among them. Two cars were in the process of being hastily aligned to block the exit. A man standing off to the side had a gun aimed at our car. Sean—it was Sean—standing like a statue, legs splayed, and holding his gun steady with two hands, like a character in a police show. Unfortunately, my head was in the way of his taking a shot at Etherington. Everything happened so quickly that it seemed like a motion picture speeded up. Etherington's jaw squared for action. I could see him mentally gauging whether he could squeeze the Mercedes through the gap between the two parked cars. I thought he might just make it. In their haste, the police had misjudged the distance.

As we passed Sean, a shot rang out. He had shot at the tire and hit it. Our car swerved dangerously, Etherington swore off a string of curses, and the next thing I knew, I was on the floor on top of Etherington, quickly checking myself out for fractures. The door on my side had caved in against me, but the impact had thrown me to the other side. Policemen came storming forward, Sean in the lead. He pulled the door open and helped me out.

His face was grim, and he looked more angry than anything else, but his voice was hollow with concern. "Are you all right?" he barked.

"Yes." His anxious anger eased visibly to relief.

One quick, fierce smile beamed, and he said, "Better get your tail out of here, honey. The fat lady hasn't sung yet."

It still wasn't over then. There was more to be done, but I was only dimly aware of all this. I was alive, and the important thing now was to discover whether Victor was. I could see Ron was all right. He had sat up and was rubbing his head. I ran down the lot, dodging cops running toward the Mercedes.

As soon as I reached Victor, I relaxed. Corpses didn't have flashing eyes and angry scowls. They didn't make frustrated, guttural sounds in their throats whether their mouths were taped shut or not. He was tied arm and leg with nylon stockings that are very hard to undo when they're pulled tightly. A policeman came and cut the nylons for me and yanked the adhesive from Victor's mouth forcefully enough so that he was rewarded with a fine Italian curse. My uncle's legs must have been cramped worse than mine. When he tried to stand up, he toppled over, and the policeman and I had to prop him up between us.

"Are you all right, Victor?" I asked, examining him for bruises, lacerations, and other signs of torture.

"I'd kill for a cigar," were the first words to leave his mouth even before he could stand unaided.

Ron struggled to his feet unsteadily, looked around, and began walking toward his Mercedes. His beautiful car had its front end and whole right side caved in beyond redemption. While I fell on Victor's breast, bawling for joy, he gave my shoulder a few pats and then ignored me. "Did they get the son-of-a-bitch?" he asked the policeman.

We looked toward the exit, and saw that they had gotten him and were even then dressing him in steel bracelets and herding him toward a car. Sean was there, the life of the party, slapping official backs and laughing. He actually coaxed a smile out of Marven. Gino was there, too. When Etherington had been pushed into the car, Marven and Sean started walking toward Victor. Ronald was there, but he didn't seem to be under arrest. He just stayed talking to other cops. Sean was wrong about Ronald then. He'd been innocent all along and had gotten his car destroyed for his efforts to help.

"I'm taking my uncle home," I said to the party in general. They all ignored me.

"Where's my violin?" Victor asked Marven.

"It's in Ronald's car," I said.

I looked at Sean, waiting for him to mention Ronald. "I'll get it," he said and left. He came back with the case and opened it. I knew he'd be looking for the transmitter, and if it was there, then Ronald was vindicated. At last Victor was allowed to fondle the Stradivarius. It was almost embarrassing, the way he ran his fingers over it, lovingly, speaking of curves and smoothness in very human, feminine terms.

"Was the bug in it?" I asked Sean in a low voice.

He shook his head in infinite satisfaction. "Nope. Old Ron isn't quite as stupid as I thought."

"He stopped Etherington from killing me," I said wanly.

"That wasn't too bright, your deciding to join the party."

"I would have been fine if it weren't for the dog."

"Something unexpected always turns up—like dogs and the car switch. Ron knew we'd be looking for Etherington's car and arranged to change with him. Having Etherington give him a knock on the head would make him look innocent, too. Later he could claim Etherington found the bug and got rid of it. I guess he thought I was as fine a gentleman as he is and would stick to my word about not doing any shooting till his friend got away. Too bad to disillusion him. Marven's taped their whole phone conversation so he knew what to expect."

"Do you feel up to giving us a statement tonight, Mr. Mazzini?" Marven asked quite respectfully.

"Why not? The sooner we get that English bastard behind bars, the better. Come to my place. I need a cigar."

Marven said a few words to his second in command and led Victor off to his car. Sean smiled at me and said, "He's going to be one disappointed man when he sees that empty humidor.

We better get him something to stick in his mouth, or he'll have a nervous breakdown."

I peered across the parking lot. "What about Ron?"

"He doesn't seem real anxious to join the party. He mentioned something about calling his lawyer and the Attorney General when I suggested he shouldn't leave town."

"He *will* leave! You can't just let him go!"

"He isn't going far," he said and tossed his head in Ron's direction. Gino had his hand on Ron's bicep, gently nudging him toward a squad car.

We walked back down the road to Sean's parked car. The predominant mood was anticlimax, not triumph. "You got tired of waiting for me, did you?" he asked.

"You knew I wouldn't stay there."

"That *was* a bit dangerous. Etherington's gun was loaded."

"I can't believe Ronald Strathroy is a crook."

"He's not as bad as lots of them. His back was against the wall. He never meant for anything to turn violent. He didn't want to hurt anybody."

"You're not making excuses for what he did? It was terrible—and to Victor, of all people."

"I feel sorry for the guy. He was pushed to take his father's place at Graymar, and he just doesn't have the brains to make money legally. His mother is an expensive lady—big front to keep up. I can see how he'd get pressured into doing what he did."

"Well I can't, and I hope Victor presses every charge in the book."

"We'll see," he said and opened the car door for me.

"Nobody's acting the way he should be!" I sulked. "I thought cops were supposed to be tough on criminals. Victor wasn't even glad to see me. All of a sudden you're on Ron Strathroy's side. And furthermore, I'd like to know how you got into Victor's apartment without a key before you followed me to Casa Loma tonight."

"I didn't."

"Aha! When you picked me up you said you didn't find me *in* the apartment. *In*! You were in, and furthermore you had a key when we got there."

"I didn't get in without a key. I got in with one."

"Well, where did you get it?"

"The doorman let me have a copy. We're old buddies by now, Hans and me. Mind you, I'm beginning to feel like the boy who cried wolf, always dragging poor Hans up to open your door and you not even having the courtesy to be dead. I had to give him a tip."

"How much?"

"On the horses—Flamboro Downs, the sulky races . . . Jeez, are you sure you've lived here for a month?"

"Sorry to disappoint you again. Next time the door's locked, I'll see if I can arrange to be mortally wounded. Bleeding to death all over the carpet. Hans would like that. You can be a hero, give me a blood transfusion. I'm O positive."

"You're A positive now. Must be—you've sucked me dry."

"Let's go. I don't want to miss Victor's story."

"You can catch it on TV. He won't miss this chance. Now about you and me, Cassie . . ." The moustache descended, looking like two slightly dilapidated toothbrushes and feeling the same. Of course, other sensations came along with it. Quite nice ones. Strong arms around me, warm fingers all over me, very corny but strikingly sincere words of love. There was something about not being able to live without me, a heart attack when he thought I was a thief, and something else about one in a million and knowing as soon as he saw me. Much too good for him. Lots of expense-paid travel, but whether a Mountie was expected to drag his wife along was not clear. I condescended to think about it.

Since we had a bit of trouble finding any cigars big and expensive enough to suit Victor, we arrived late for his story. Marven was just leaving. He had the violin case under his arm which threw Victor into a frenzy. My uncle wasn't too reluctant to begin his story over again. He was working up to a dramatic presentation for the mass media. He'd changed out of his rumpled suit into a flamboyant, burgundy colored dressing gown made of some patterned material related to satin. He had an ascot at his neck and was preening in front of a mirror.

"Who's this, another cop?" he asked when we entered. He already had a stogie in his hand. He must have made Marven stop on the way home.

"This is Sean Bradley, Victor," I said. "He's a Mountie."

"My name's John Weiss," Sean corrected.

"Right, I forgot," I said.

"Lloyd's of London," Sean added.

"Lloyd's!" That was me, shrieking. "What about the scarlet tunic! And the funny hat?"

"Don't mind her, she's an idiot," Victor explained. "Phone your mother, Cassie. She'll be worried sick."

"She'll be sound asleep. I'll phone her tomorrow, and I am not an idiot. Anything you two have to say, I plan to hear and object to."

"She will, you know," Victor cautioned, but he wore an approving smile. Whether at John, who I went on calling Sean for a few days, or the fact that I had done the right thing for an Italian niece and found a mate, I wasn't sure. I don't even know how he knew I'd landed John, but being Italian, he sensed it.

"You can't be an insurance agent," I objected. "Lloyd's is in London!"

"That's where I work out of. Parelli's the Mountie," John explained. I remembered those shirts with English labels in his hotel room. "Gino Parelli. He's a special agent with the RCMP. I'm with Lloyd's. We both wanted the same thing and worked together."

"Why did you call yourself Sean Bradley? Insurance agents don't have to change their names."

"The famous ones do," Victor told me. "According to Marven, John here is famous, in his own way. Sorry I didn't recognize you, John. All Marven told me was your name. And you're just the man I want to talk to. You can't reason with the police. They're just here to arrest people." I didn't trust the gleam in his eyes.

"If you're trying to arrange a deal about Strathroy, it's the cops you want, not me," John cautioned. "Of course, I'm interested in anything you might have to suggest. Do you think Strathroy might be willing to hand over the rest of the Carpani take, arrange a deal for some clemency consideration?"

"I don't give a damn about that milksop," Victor said. "Lock him up and throw away the key for all I care. It's the violin I'm interested in."

"Did you get your money back?" I asked.

"Just like her mother," Victor repined. "I got it back. Or will—as soon as they no longer need it for evidence. About the violin, Mr. Weiss—John. How do you plan to return it to the contessa?"

"I'll take it personally."

Victor's fingers were nervously massaging his chin. I had a little trouble leading him back to tell us his ordeal but not too much. He made a very good rant of it, like a ham actor in an afternoon soap, but there wasn't much new. I already knew about his having met Etherington at a party, about buying the violin, going to Bitwell, and so on.

"Where did they take you? Where have you been all this time?" I asked.

"Locked up in a damned little cramped bungalow Etherington lives in out in the boonies. Some place called Port Credit. It was only a stone's throw from that mall where they dumped me tonight. He kept me doped half the time but let me wake up long enough to go to the can and eat, occasionally. Beans and eggs. Not even a dish of pasta. And my cigars, the son-of-a-bitch smoked them in front of me and wouldn't let me have a puff. Imagine, being low and petty enough to steal a man's cigars. Imported!"

"Easy on the sons-of-bitches, Victor. The language I mean, not Etherington."

He glanced at me impatiently and went on talking. "Somebody—well it was Strathroy, I know that now, though I didn't at the time—Strathroy took my cigars while he was rifling my apartment for the violin and brought them to the hut. He meant them for me, but that goddamm'd—"

"Easy on the goddams, too."

"You want to think twice before marrying this one," Victor advised John. Then his caution was awakened to the occasion, and he tried to rectify his error. "Of course, she's really not a bad sort of girl."

"That's half the trouble right there," John agreed.

"Tell us about being locked up," I ordered.

"They didn't torture me unless you can call hours of Lawrence Welk torture. What upset their little applecart is that I didn't knuckle under and tell them where I hid the Stradivarius. Clever, eh?" he congratulated himself. "Those two are rank amateurs. They didn't know what to do with me once they kidnapped me. That wasn't a part of the plan. Etherington panicked when I went to the conservatory and found out the violin was stolen. He knew it would be all over the papers by morning. He was following me from the moment I left him. He grabbed me at gunpoint in my garage."

"But you'd already escaped him and hidden the violin at the Casa Loma," I said.

"Yes, and put some sneakers in the case. If they managed to grab it, I didn't want it to feel empty. I carried the case down to Union Station to fool him, but the amateur lost me in traffic. He was waiting for me back at the apartment garage. The phone calls were flying thick and fast to Strathroy, asking what he should do. Of course, he didn't use Ron's name. They have some other—some sucker lined up to buy a necklace and were shaking in their boots in case the whole Carpani story came out and blew their scam into the headlines. I'd told Etherington I was keeping it a secret that I'd gotten hold of the old Italian violin till I had it in tune. We weren't calling it a Strad then though we both knew."

"Just as you thought, Sean—John," I congratulated. "There is one other thing, Victor. Why did you hide your Guarneri in the locker?"

"You found that, did you? Where is it?"

"In your studio. And you didn't answer the question."

"I needed it for the performance at Roy Thomson that evening. But first I needed the case to protect the Stradivarius, so I had to leave my own fiddle at home. You don't leave a Guarneri sitting on display in a car for some crook to steal. I planned to dart back and pick it up before I went down to the hall. Rather than having to take the elevator up to the apartment to get it, I decided to stick it in the locker. It'd save time."

"I see."

"Now quit interrupting. Where was I? Oh, yes, I was telling you about Etherington. He's posing as a gentleman down on his luck," he continued. "When they kidnapped a famous person like Mazzini, they knew they were in over their necks and didn't dare harm me. I told them, lay a finger on me, and you're a marked man. They think I have friends in the mob.

And between the two of them, they couldn't find the violin," he crowed.

"I found it, though," I said and received not a single nod of approval.

"As I said, John," Victor continued, "it's the violin I'm really interested in. Do you think the contessa would consider selling it?"

"It's a family heirloom. She was very upset about losing it," John told him doubtfully.

"Good looking woman, is she?"

"Not bad."

"How old?"

"The right side of forty. Red-haired, full-figured lady, very stylish."

The more John talked, the wider Victor's smile grew. "A Balzacian figure. A real woman," he beamed. "And a widow, I understand?"

"For a few years now."

"What's her phone number? What time is it in Italy? Is it too early to call? Cassie, is there any pasta in the house? Make me some spaghetti. This woman can't make gnocchi or fettucini to save her soul," he added aside to John.

"I'll give it a try," John offered.

Victor was much too excited to go to bed. He kept popping his head into the kitchen, as often as not catching John and myself simmering, but not pasta. "CBC is sending over a reporter at eight tomorrow morning," he announced on one trip.

Later it was, "The *Globe* and the *Star* both want exclusives, Cassie. Which shall I give the honor? Exclusive be damned, I'll let them all come, including the *Sun*. I hope you saved all the papers. There should have been good coverage."

I assured him they were all awaiting his perusal. The next time he came, he had dragged the manager of Roy Thomson Hall from his bed and had gotten a promise of a new concert series. "This one will be a sellout," he crooned. "They'll be lined up for tickets as if I were a rock star. I'll make real music popular for the masses. More garlic," he added without even tasting the spaghetti sauce.

When the spaghetti was ready, Victor opened some of his

best red wine, and we sat down to celebrate. We heard a great
deal more self-congratulating from Victor about how he had
handled his incarceration, and his plans to have the story
ghost-written into a best seller. "*The Vanishing Violinist* I'll
call it. No, that sounds like Perry Mason, and I'll want my
name in there. *Mazzini Is Missing*—make that *The Great
Mazzini Is Missing*. That has a nice ring to it. Speaking of ring,
I can call the contessa now," he said, glancing at his watch.

I was a little suspicious when he went into his bedroom to
make the call. Once he got the contessa on the line, however,
he became so excited that his voice carried through the walls.
He spoke in Italian, along the following lines:

"My dear contessa, I hope I haven't gotten you out of
bed? . . . Oh, having lunch? Terribly sorry. I'm calling from
Canada and didn't realize, but I have good news for you. I've
found your violin. . . . It's fine, I guarded it with my life—
literally. I've been held captive and tortured for days. . . .
Oh, I'll live. Kind of you to ask. . . . A wonderful instrument, the finest violin I've ever played. . . . Do I play? Ha
ha, I forgot to introduce myself. This is Victor Mazzini
speaking. (a very gratified little laugh) *Grazie*. Yes, the one
they call the Great Mazzini. I'm surprised you've heard of me
all the way in Italy! I'm flattered. Yes, a native son. . . . Too
kind. No, really! *All* my records? You're making me blush,
Contessa. Oh, very soon, you'll have it very soon. I insist on
taking it to you personally. We don't want some bourgeois
insurance agent taking it, using it for a doorstop. (I smiled
apologetically at John.) Not at all, a pleasure. . . . Well,
there is one little thing. If you could put up with its absence for
another month. Oh, the very best care! I'll hire a special guard
to watch it. And a violin needs to be played, you know. But
then I don't mean to tell *you* anything about violins. . . . A
concert series. The world deserves to hear the great Carpani
Stradivarius. I'll send you a copy of the record. Including a
little surprise. . . . Don't like surprises? What an unusual
lady. Well, if you insist, it's the little piece I wrote to honor the
Carpani Strad. . . . I write a little, I'm not a serious composer. I call it unofficially *Capriccio Carpani*—a capricious
little thing, just in fun, you know. Very modern and youthful."

"There goes my song," I said to John.

Victor continued his fawning conversation. "Stay at your villa? That sounds charming, Contessa. No, I'll be alone. I'm an old bachelor. . . . (Another delighted laugh) If you insist then, a *young* bachelor. Perhaps your husband and I . . . Ah, forgive me, I didn't know. . . . (His tone vibrated with sympathy) Yes, I know all about loneliness, that's nothing new to me. But I have a much better idea! Why don't you come to Toronto and see the concert live? Let me make the arrangements. I insist."

John and I exchanged a disbelieving stare.

"Why don't we arrange it by letter then? And my dear Contessa . . . Maria? Charming! Could a bachelor be very forward and ask you to enclose a picture of yourself? You have the advantage on me. I have no idea what you look like, but if your beauty matches your lovely voice, I shall be the envy of North America."

There were a few more crooning murmurs, too subdued to make it through the door. "Where's Gino?" I asked John.

"I imagine he's consummating a life insurance policy next door, right about now. No, seriously, he said someone should explain to Mrs. Friske what's been going on and volunteered to do it."

"Beat you to it, huh?"

In a minute Victor came out rubbing his hands in glee. "It's done. She's coming, and until she gets here, she'll send you a letter giving you permission for me to keep the Stradivarius till she arrives. Meanwhile, I'll be playing it at my next concert."

I knew that look. "Meanwhile" would be as long as he lived. By hook or crook, he'd end up with the Carpani Strad if he had to marry the Contessa to get it. But for the present, he was content to phone Marven and demand its return.

The next move was to look after his other girlfriend, Eleanor Strathroy. John, whose only interest was in saving his insurance company money, aided and abetted him every step of the way. It wasn't done in a morning, especially with so many interviews to be conducted. The affair couldn't be kept entirely silent, but with cooperation from Victor and the Contessa in not pressing charges, with the remainder of the haul from her villa returned, with Ronald's "resignation" from Graymar and

Eleanor's selling her mansion to pay off his debts, it passed
into history with hardly a ripple, and with no jail term for
Ronald. Mr. Etherington was brought to nominal justice on a
former crime—three months is what he actually got—but the
big losers were the Strathroys even if it wasn't legal justice.

They are consigned to the suburbs in an area east of Toronto
called Scarborough but more familiarly known as Scarberia. A
fate worse than death for them. I give it a year, maximum,
before Eleanor finds either a rich husband for herself or a rich
bride for Ronald. One should feel some outrage, I suppose, but
it's hard to be outraged when you've just gotten engaged. I
have more important things to do, like talk John into shaving
off his moustache, take him to a decent tailor, and convince
Mom he'll be a good husband even if he isn't Italian.

My visions still occur. I see us walking by the Seine,
hand-in-hand, smiling at the chestnut trees and water. I see us
in John's flat in London, receiving frantic calls to dash off to
Rome, New York, Paris, having to cancel the duchess's dinner
invitation. I see myself in designer labels, solving baffling
cases. I think John sees me in a frilly apron, waving him off
from behind the white picket fence while he solves the crimes.
Or perhaps he's come to know me better than that. We
sybarites must have a little excitement, as well as our material
pleasure, and his career offers considerable scope in that
direction. It is, after all, the very wealthy who have their
diamonds and things stolen. Perhaps my visions are slightly
exaggerated, but I enjoy them for all that, as I have every
intention of enjoying the reality of a two-by-four life with
John. *C'est la vie.*